Red Dirt Girls

by

Carolyn Haywood

Prologue

Sophia

Mama always called us red dirt girls and the way she said it, well, I wasn't sure if it was a good thing or a bad thing. But Cousin Pearl said it was what we were made of. She said we were tough and had stick-to-itiveness and if the right seeds were planted we would grow up strong and as valuable as the tobacco we planted in the lower field. I figured that made us special cause that tobacco was like gold.

We were special, all right, and we were tough, only cause we had to be. When I was fifteen, Cousin Pearl gave me a taped and tied up old J.C. Penny shoebox filled with what she said were the things I would need in the future. Things that would bring me comfort and closure and understanding. I shoved that old box as far back in the closet as I could and erased it from my memory. I didn't want any comfort or closure or understanding. I just wanted to forget, and I did.

It's Spring and time to clean out the old and give the new a place to grow, so I have been working diligently on decluttering. My first task was the old blanket chest that used to be Mama's, and her Mama's, and her Mama's and so forth. It's stained brown, with dark circles of oil from the kerosene lamps that used to sit on it and it is so old the hinges have worn out more than once and now the top just sits there, one hinge dangling. I wonder who made it, for it is certainly handmade, rough and primitive, worn smooth not from sandpaper but from the relentless hands of all the Mamas who have lovingly stored their most precious treasures there: baby clothes, christening dresses, funeral shrouds. I've hauled that thing around, first to Cousin Pearl's, then to college, to my first apartment and my second and it finally came to rest in the spare bedroom of my latest house. In all that hauling, not once have I opened it, but this morning I did and I found the old shoebox in a cloud of must, beneath layers of neatly folded scrap quilts hand stitched by Grandma Rita. The masking tape was gone but the orange residue was still there, and the tobacco string holding it together was as strong as ever.

I will admit that I was disappointed when I finally opened the lid of that box. I don't know what I expected, maybe some shining ray of light to spring out and hit me in the face, some instant knowledge or acute awareness. Something. Anything. Instead, I saw it was just a box of old pictures and old letters, a few receipts and scribbled notes. The collection of a past life, one I had moved on from and did not want to go back to. The pictures on the top were of me and my sisters and Cousin Pearl, in faded color. I sifted through them to the older black and white photos and pulled out one of Grandma Rita. She is so unimaginably young. Thin, a wisp, separated from girlhood only by a wedding ring. Her hair is lush and stylish and I can imagine it shining and bouncing as she moves in the sun. She is wearing lipstick, red, I am sure and a crisp apron over a floral dress. The photographer has caught her by surprise, her mouth open, eyes wide and her hand stopped in travel midway to her face. She looks like she has been laughing, as if she has been caught being happy. My heart hurts for this girl and I am taken aback at the intensity of my feelings. But then, I know her story. I wonder if my mother has been born yet and turn the picture hoping to see a date but there is none.

In another picture, I see a young man dressed in denim overalls proudly standing beside an Indian motorcycle. Shoulders back, straight, chin tucked. Uncle Joe, who I never knew, it must be, and it is, so says the back. He is handsome, with a devilish smile and the same twinkle in his eye that his mother has. I can just see the corner of the house behind him and notice that the paint has chipped away in places and the rot has settled in. Oh, the foretelling, the shadowing it shows! I hold the picture closer and rub my thumb over Uncle Joe's face. His eyes are green, I know it, like my eyes, like Mama's, like Grandma's. It is the color of my family and marks us like a genetic brand. I wonder if there is a sadness behind that twinkle or some deep, ominous message and I wait for him to blink and show me, but the camera cannot tell me that. It can only reveal the happiness of this single moment and I relish that, in my mind, because of this picture, Uncle Joe will forever be happy.

Here is a picture of Grandpa Joe sitting on his dusty, barely red anymore, Farmall tractor. He is grizzled and unkempt with a half smile, cigarette smoke curling in front of his face, daring the camera to catch his image. I think he may be a handsome man, but I can't tell. His hair is curly and wet with sweat, combed back with his fingers; I don't think for the picture, but so he can see the furrows in front of him. From the shadow of the tractor, the sun is low and Grandpa Joe must be tired. He works a shift at the mill and a shift on the farm after that. The cigarette is clenched tightly in the unsmiling side of his mouth and his eyes are squinched, almost shut. I imagine they are dark, so very dark, and intense, maybe even brooding, and it scares me. I throw the picture back in the box, quickly, like I have been burned.

And here, finally, is my mother, Lillian, with Cousin Pearl, arms locked around each other's back, heads tilted toward each other, smiling. Best friends, still girls, knock-kneed. Mama in a faded and frayed dress, Cousin Pearl, snappy and stylish.

I am not prepared for the tears that wet my cheeks. I quickly wipe them away, lay the picture beside me, and dig through the box again. My fingers wrap around a smaller box, much smaller than I remember, but then I was only a girl when I last clutched it to my chest. I cannot stop the tears or the sobs that follow. I feel like a cliche. The weight of the world has been lifted from my shoulders, the fog has lifted and I can see clearly now, the clouds have parted and the sun is shining brightly on my face. Bless her heart, Cousin Pearl was right again.

Book 1

############### CHAPTER 1 ################

The Indian

1962

Red and Orange. These are the colors of the dirt, the leaves, and the heavy late afternoon air. The newly plowed fields are dressed in shades of these colors, the ridges rough with small clods of clay, bits of tobacco stems, and now and then an arrowhead. The furrows are straight and deep like the first impressions you get of the people who live here. If it were morning, the fields would be sparkling with the dew reflecting off the multitude of spiderwebs, like a field of diamonds in a fairy tale, but it is afternoon, a hot, hazy afternoon in the fall, and the red dust stirred up by a rumbling old school bus sticks to anything it touches, staining it forever, like the bus itself, once yellow, now a hybrid dusty orange.

Inside the bus, the kids bump and slide, talking and laughing, happy to be going home. They don't care about the dust, don't see the dinginess of their clothes or their lives. They are kids, after all, happy with the little things, like the thrill they get when the bus hits a pothole, and their thin bodies bounce high off the seats that are too stiff and slick to hold them down. Lillian Dunn, just twelve, and her cousin Pearl sit in the back holding onto the bar of the seat in front of them singing the sad tale of Tom Dooley. Lillian, too thin and spare, fair-haired and fair-skinned sings louder than her dark haired cousin and slightly off key. But she is jubilant and contagious, and she makes everyone around her smile. Her handsome brother, Little Joe, the bus driver, steals glances in the rear view mirror at the singing girls. He is protective of his little sister and winces each time she hits a sour note. Such a strange morbid tale for two young girls to be singing.

> Hang down your head, Tom Dooley
> Hang down your head and cry

> Hang down your head, Tom Dooley
> Poor boy, you're bound to die
> Met her on the mountain
> There I took her life
> Met her on the mountain
> Stabbed her with my knife

Like the red dirt, they don't notice the tragedy in the words. All the songs they know are catchy tunes with doggone hard life living lyrics. Lovin' and dyin' and cheatin' and killin' and sometimes trying find something to eat or maybe getting a job or keeping one. This is what they expect from life, and they don't see the sadness in that, just the joy they feel in singing with each other.

Little Joe slows the bus to a stop at a plain one-story farmhouse with a steep roof and a deep porch running across the front. An Arts and Crafts style bungalow they call it, with the original paint faded and missing on the siding, while rot has claimed the edges of the porch floorboards. The red dirt fields surrounding the house are sloppy with the remnants of tobacco plants, leafless stalks still waiting for the plow to turn them under. It's a tired and wanting family farm, but Lillian calls it home.

Pearl jumps off the bus first, Lillian aching to jump too, but Little Joe swings out his arm and stops her before she can even get to the step.

"Hey, Sis. Tell Mama I'm gonna be late for supper."

"What you gonna do?"

Lillian stomps her foot, the one with the untied shoestring, and puts her free hand on her hips, sassing and teasing her older brother.

"Go see Caaaathy?"

She puckers her lips and makes kissing noises at Little Joe, knowing this will embarrass him but not caring.

"No such luck, kiddo." He blushes and winks. "I'm gonna see an Indian. Don't tell Mama or Daddy."

He glances at Pearl and puts his finger to his mouth, bouncing it off his lips with each word.

"And don't you either, Little Bit."

Pearl shakes her head, solemn now, and proud to be the keeper of a secret from her second favorite cousin.

"I won't tell, I promise."

Little Joe places his hand on the gear shift, letting Lillian pass. Impatiently, she jumps off the bus from the second step, flying through the air, just for a moment though, before landing next to Pearl.

"Me, either."

She locks her arm with Pearl's and the two girls start singing again, skipping in unison down the long, rocky driveway, joined by the young blue tick hound dog, Gideon, who follows them home every day, bounding like the big puppy he is and joining in with the singing, howling, for he is part of this singing group.

> This time tomorrow
> Reckon where I'll be
> Down in some lonesome valley
> Hanging from a white oak tree

Rita Dunn checks the biscuits in the white porcelain electric oven. She leans in too close and the heat curls the little wisps of hair that have escaped from the bun on the back of her head. Beads of sweat roll down her forehead. She dabs at them with her mama's feed sack apron.

"Lord have mercy. It's November, for Pete's sake." She says to the biscuits.

The electric oven and the fridge are antiques, handed down from her sister when Little Joe was just a baby. Rita prefers to use the wood stove for cooking but it is too hot for a fire so she has had to make do with the "new" stove.

"That you, Lillian?"

Rita calls absently from the kitchen, knowing for sure it's her, but compelled by habit to ask anyway.

"Is Pearl with you? Come on in here and give me a hand."

"We're coming, Mama"

Rita looks too old for her age. Dark puffy moons color her cheeks, just below her green, green, so very green, but still twinkling eyes. Her face droops like she is too tired for this world. She is faded and careworn, like the apron that is tied tightly holding the waist of the limp and sagging dress in place. With a deep and resigned sigh, she stirs the beans bubbling on the stove.

Lillian pops into the doorway first, Pearl just behind. Both girls slam their school books on the scarred, wooden kitchen table.

"Beans again, Mama? Why do we always have to have beans?"

Rita turns, hands on hips, eyes snapping now at her sassy daughter. It's too hot for this nonsense, she thinks. What kind of girl am I raising?

"Why, Lillian Dunn! Shame on you for not being grateful for what we have. Run out to the canning house and get a jar of that pepper relish you like so much. Maybe that'll help you be more thankful."

Lillian does not feel shamed. What she said is true. Beans and cornbread and sometimes biscuits all the time. She's too young to realize she's as poor as she is. She runs out the back door, shouting as she slams the screen door.

"Beans, beans, good for the heart."

And softer now as she nears the canning house.

"The more you eat, the more you fart."

Rita pulls frosty ice trays from the small freezer compartment in the refrigerator and hands them to Pearl. Her life is full of these little habits. She knows Pearl will fill the glasses without having to be asked. Lillian, though, is as different as she can be. The good Lord knows she has to be told every single thing, and then reminded several times.

"Honestly, I don't understand that girl, Pearl. Is she that way at school?"

Pearl nods her head as she cracks the ice trays, dumping the ice into a mustard colored pottery bowl.

"She just likes to have fun, Aunt Rita, picking at you. She doesn't really mean to be sassy."

Rita reaches into a white metal cabinet, pulls out five mismatched glasses and sets them on the table so Pearl can put the ice in them.

"Well, I wish she'd learn to be more of a young lady. Always running and always talking back. Lord knows I've tried and tried."

She pours the tea, thick and swirling with sugar, from a large enamel pitcher into the glasses. Pearl distributes them around the table, careful to put the large one at the head where Joe sits.

"How's my sister doing? She like that new washer your daddy got for her?"

"Oh, yes! She loves it. She won't use that dryer, though. She says the clothes don't smell right, and don't feel right either."

There is a red-rimmed white enamel tub in the large country sink, full of bubbly, soapy water and Rita washes a dirty pot as if her life depends on it. She stares out the window, watching the sun as it sits low on the horizon.

"Well, it's the sun that really does the cleaning. Bleaches even in the folds of the wrinkles and, well, you just can't get any better a smell than sun dried sheets. That's what I think, anyway."

The screen door slams again and Lillian bounds in with a mason jar of red, green and yellow hot pepper jelly. The sound startles Rita and she jumps, dropping the bowl into the water.

"Honey, please don't slam that door. How many times do I have to tell you? It's barely on there as it is. Get the plates and y'all set the table."

Rita sends a worried look out the kitchen window and speaks softly to herself. It's just not like him to be so late. Like her, he is a creature of habit and he can always be relied upon to do what he says he will do, to be where he says he will be. He's a good boy.

"Where is Little Joe?"

Lillian and Pearl, now setting the silverware beside the plates, steal knowing glances at each other and smile. Rita doesn't notice because her attention is drawn to the stewing meat. She gives it a quick stir with a battered, well used wooden spoon, and blowing first on the hot meat, takes a large bite. She nods her head. It's just about done.

"Little Joe say anything to you?"

"He said to tell you he'd be late for supper. Drove off plumb before I had a chance to ask him why".

The lie slips out smoothly from Lillian's lips, not a hint given and Rita is sure, now, that something must be wrong with Little Joe.

"Why, that's not like him, not at all"

She checks on the biscuits again, worry lining her face. They've risen high and flakey but the golden brown crust they're supposed to have is just a light tan drawn around the edge of each one.

"I reckon we can wait a few more minutes."

She salts the beef, pours it into an earthenware bowl, places it on the table, and covers it with a thin white dish cloth. She smooths back her hair and her apron, straightens her back and holds her head high, determined not to worry about her beloved son. Still, she can't help but sneak a glance out the window again, and there, she sees, despite her worry, is Little Joe.

"What in the world…"

She rushes to the kitchen sink and leans closer to the window, puzzled.

"Why, I'll be. What's Little Joe doing with that motorcycle?"

In a burst of pent up excitement, Lillian jumps and hollers. She grabs Pearl's hand and they run out the kitchen door, and head to the side yard, Rita following close behind.

Little Joe, pride beaming a halo around him, holds the handle bar of a '49 Indian motorcycle while his daddy, Joe, inspects it. Joe is spare and lean, like his wife, but has a rough edge. Smoke and drink form the deep lines in his face. His overalls are covered in the red dust kicked up by the faded Farmall tractor just behind him. He looks at his son.

"It's a nice one, I reckon. Where'd…"

"Is it yours?"

Lillian and Pearl interrupt loudly as they run to the cedar tree. Lillian gets to the motorcycle first and grabs a handlebar with one hand, rubbing the cracked leather seat with the other. She's never seen anything so magnificent in all her young years. And to think that Little Joe owns this is just about overwhelming. If only, no, of course, he will let Lillian ride.

"Can we go for a ride?"

"Oh, please, please, please! Me, too." begs Pearl.

Both girls hold hands, hug each other and jump up and down, unable to contain the wonder that Little Joe has a real motorcycle.

Joe pulls a dirty rag from his back pocket and wipes his hands and face before returning it to its place. He wants to know where Little Joe got the motorcycle but the squealing girls are just too much for him right now. And besides, he's hot and hungry and he wants a glass of cold sweet tea real bad.

"Now just hold on there, girls. Mama's been in there cookin' all afternoon…"

"Oh my gosh! The biscuits! They'll be burned to a crisp!"

Rita turns and runs to the house. Joe looks at the girls.

"There you go. I say we go on in there and have our supper. Then, if Little Joe feels like it, maybe he'll take us for a ride. What do y'all say?"

He winks at Little Joe.

"I say, I sure am hungry! Come on, girls. Let's eat."

He puts his arms around both girls and gives them a squeeze. Lillian is disappointed, but as sure as the sun coming up that they will get to ride after supper. Little Joe never lies. He loves her so. She knows it.

The family sits around the table set with a simple but plentiful meal: beans seasoned with side meat, stewed beef, hot pepper jelly, a mound of biscuits and thick rounds of homemade butter. Joe passes the bowl of biscuits.

"Sure looks good, Mama."

"Thank you, Joe. Little Joe, will you do the honors?"

They join hands as Little Joe leads them in the blessing.

"Our Father, we thank you for this wonderful supper and for the good woman who fixed it…"

He glances up and across the table at his mother who returns the look with a smile.

"Oh, and thank you for Mr. McDowel who was kind enough to sell me the motorcycle. Amen."

Lillian and Pearl can't help but giggle with all the excitement.

"AMEN!"

Rita picks up her fork and looks expectantly at Little Joe.

"Well?"

"Well, what?"

Little Joe is a tease and a natural born storyteller.

"Joseph Dunn! You know very well what. However did you come home with that motorcycle?"

Before he begins his tale, Little Joe looks solemnly at each and every person at the table. Lillian is bubbling with excitement, eyes twinkling, Pearl listening intensely and patiently, Rita worrying and fidgety, Joe stone-faced.

"Well, Y'all remember when I was fourteen, Daddy told me I could have a car if I earned the money to buy it. But what I really wanted was that Indian motorcycle so I went straight over to Mr. McDowell's and convinced him to sell me that motorcycle."

Little Joe scoops up a forkful of beef and chews patiently and slowly, making the others wait, on purpose.

"He agreed to sell it to me for $500. Even better, he said I could pay him whenever I was able for the next three years and he would keep it till I paid him in full."

"But that was two years ago, not three." Pearl interrupts.

"That's good figuring there sweet Pearl." He pinches her chin.

"When I went to pay him today, he looked me straight in the eye and told me he didn't want any more money. He said he figured I'd need all my spare cash to keep her running, and he also figured that since I was sixteen, I might be needing that motorcycle right now. I allowed that he was right. Then he said that he figured as I was an honorable man, I wouldn't be averse to a new deal."

He pauses again for a few bites of biscuit.

"These sure are good, Mama."

"Honestly, Little Joe. You're just like your granddaddy! For Heaven's sake, tell us what the new deal is!"

Little Joe grins. He's got his daddy's half grin, lopsided smile. He picks up his fork and plays with his food.

"The new deal is this. I'm to work for him every Saturday for the next six months."

He sits back and looks at all the happy, loving faces surrounding him.

"And Mama. He said he knew I was honorable and raised right cause you were my Mama."

Rita gets flustered and pleased all at once, but Joe stabs at his food and glares at her. He doesn't have green eyes like his wife but he does have the little monster that stirs his memory and his emotions. Lillian leans over to Pearl and whispers.

"Mr. McDowell is Mama's old boyfriend."

Rita puts her fork down forcefully on the table, angry at her daughter for speaking gossip and worried about the effect it will have on her husband. Her weak-minded, insecure husband.

"That was a long time ago, Lillian Dunn, and has nothing to do with now. Mr. McDowell was, and always has been, a generous and kind man. I'm pleased to think that after all these years he still thinks well of me."

She is nervous, afraid she will say the wrong thing, but steadfast and she looks hard into Little Joe's eyes.

"Little Joe got his motorcycle because of his hard work and diligence to a debt he owed, not because of a crush a boy had on me when I was just a girl."

No one speaks. No one knows what to say. Except Lillian, who laughs, like she always does, breaking the rising tension around the table.

"Well, I don't know about y'all, but I'm ready to ride on Little Joe's motorcycle. Lord knows, it's gotta be more fun than Daddy's old truck!"

With that, she stands up.

"Well?"

Little Joe pushes back his rickety, ladder back chair.

"Let's go then."

Moments later, Little Joe sits on the motorcycle with Lillian in front of him. He expertly spins the bike around toward the sunset and flies down the road, Gideon, bounding and barking behind. Joe, Rita, and Pearl watch as the two get smaller and smaller, further and further away from home.

Little Joe hollers at his sister.

"Hold on Lil Sis, cause we're gonna ride the wind."

Sophia

Ride the wind. I had forgotten that phrase. On purpose, perhaps, to forget, maybe. Who knows. But now that I remember, I think of Mama, the wind in her hair, her face forward, eyes looking ahead, loving arms taking her to a future filled with excitement, riding the wind and going wherever it blows. A moment in time when life was euphoric. But the sun was setting, not rising and perhaps that made a difference in the secret rules of the universe.

*************** CHAPTER 2 ***************

Perfect Harmony is Not for All

1962

It is night, the darkness punctuated by the light of so many stars, the bright moon, and the dim light coming from the room of Rita and Joe. Little Joe, Lillian, and Pearl sit in the old straight back chairs on the front porch singing country songs, Little Joe strumming his 1933 sunburst Gibson guitar. Perfect harmony between him and Pearl with Lillian leading in pure emotional and heartfelt vocals. Gideon, lies comfortably curled in front of the screen door, leaving the singing to the kids for the night.

When the song ends, Little Joe hands the guitar to Pearl.

"Your turn, sweet Pearl. Think you can remember?"

Pearl takes the guitar and holds it close, for it is a precious object to her.

"Oh, yes!"

She adjusts her grip and plays without missing a beat.

> You are my Sunshine, my only Sunshine
> You make me happy when skies are gray
> You'll never know, dear, how much I love you
> Please don't take my Sunshine away

Little Joe claps and whistles at the end of the song. He is so very proud of his talented little cousin. A natural, he thinks.

"Well, I'll say, Miss Pearl, if you ain't something else. How'd you remember them chords?"

Pearl hands the guitar back to him and with all the earnestness of a twelve-year old, appeals to him.

"I want to play read bad. I practice in my sleep. I practice with a pretend guitar. Look…"

She holds an imaginary guitar and plays pretend chords, her face straining for all the world like she is really playing.

"I'm going to be a Country and Western singer, just like Patsy Cline."

Not to be outdone, Lillian stands up and pipes in loudly.

"Yeah, and I'm gonna be an actress like Marilyn Monroe. We're gonna leave this crummy ole red dirt farm and I AIN'T comin' back. Besides, I got a part in the school play so I'm as good as on my way."

She strikes a Marilyn Monroe pose, pursing her lips and fluffing her hair with one hand. She giggles at her silly self and Pearl joins in.

Little Joe reaches out to Pearl for his guitar and she gives it back to him reluctantly.

"You just leave then little missy. I ain't going nowhere. I'm going to stay right here and plant my feet in this dirt. Just like that ole cedar tree over yonder."

"We'll just see, won't we?" Lillian is sassy to everyone, even her beloved brother.

"I reckon we will". He turns his attention to Pearl.

"All right then, Pearl. How bout this one."

He plays "John Hardy", another old favorite.

"Now this is a new chord."

Little Joe demonstrates the chord and turns the guitar over to Pearl. She easily imitates him and again, he is impressed with her natural ability. Like a duck to water, he thinks. It's so easy for her.

"I'll tell you what, Little Bit. You keep that guitar for a while and practice. You know, maybe if your daddy sees what you can do, he'll get you one of your own."

Pearl bursts into tears at the kindness of this gesture.

"Hey, I didn't mean to make you cry."

She gets up and hugs his neck, her face wet with tears.

"Thank you, Little Joe. I'll learn to play real good, I promise."

"I know you will, Little Bit. Hey, why don't you stop that crying and sing something."

Pearl dries her eyes, sits back down and the three begin a new song.

The music carries throughout the house and into the bedroom where Rita, dressed for bed sits at her worn out vanity brushing her hair, peaceful and enjoying the sounds of her children. She doesn't care that the vanity is old. It was her grandmother's and she remembers watching her sit just like this, brushing her long, long grey hair, her reflection smiling at Rita with those so green eyes. She imagines herself her grandmother's age and her grandchildren sitting on the same bed watching her at the same vanity with the same green eyes and she is overflowing with love.

"I'm so proud of Little Joe."

Joe, dressed in a white tee shirt and crisp ironed boxers, sits on the edge of the bed, smoking a cigarette and enjoying the breeze coming in from the open window.

"He's a pretty good ole boy. I reckon I'm proud of him, too."

He takes a final puff and puts the cigarette butt out in the overflowing glass ashtray.

"I just hope he's smart enough to get the hell outta this place one day."

"Well, I hope he stays right here, marries that little Cathy, and has a whole house full of young'uns."

Joe gets off the bed, agitated, and stands behind Rita, looking at her sullenly in the mirror. He wants something for his son, something more than the life he has, but he doesn't exactly know what and that disturbs him.

"You got the girl for that. That's all she's good for anyway."

Rita stands up and puts her hands on Joe's shoulders, trying to soothe him, to pacify him.

"She's just a young girl, Joe. A dreamer. She'll settle her mind in a few years."

"You spoil her, letting her run like a wild thing. She should be doing chores, helping out. God knows there's plenty of doing that needs to be done around here."

He pushes her away and grabs his pants from the back of the chair in the bedroom and quickly puts them on. All this talk.

"I'm going out."

"Joe. Please." Rita can't hide her alarm.

"It's late. Come to bed. Please, Honey, take off your pants and come to bed."

Rita follows him as he goes out the door, pleading, begging but he is already gone. The day has been too much for him, too taxing, what with the heat, and the motorcycle and the talk of Sean McDowell.

"Please don't go, Joe."

Over the sound of the music and singing, she hears the rumble of the old truck as it rolls over the river rock driveway. The kids don't notice he is leaving and she is relieved that their evening is not spoiled. She folds back the chenille bedspread, neatly draping it over the footboard of the bed and revealing the quilt she helped her grandmother piece together when she was a little girl. Here is a star, made from a housedress of Mema's and here, a triangle of PawPaw's shirt. She rubs her hand over a square of calico, all that is left of her girlhood. A favorite dress, worn only on Sundays, and let down each year until she was too big to let it out anymore. How wise Mema was to save it in this quilt so she could treasure it forever. How much love there is here.

How funny life is, she thinks. Who will know this quilt, a thing, a living thing, kept alive with memories. Will it die when she does, lost in time? She herself can barely remember some of the fabric and most she imagines, are from Mema's past and her mother's past and maybe even before them, like the quilts in the old blanket chest. Who knows what life they led before they were cut into pieces and made into something else entirely. Like life itself, like her life.

She removes her robe and lies down on the bed in between the sheets that smell like sunshine and she is comforted. Maybe she should make a quilt with Lillian. What a thought, that she'd ever be that still. Maybe Joe will come home sober. Maybe Lillian will stay whole.

############### CHAPTER 3 ###############

The Talent Show

Saturday morning arrives cool with bright blue skies, a blessed relief from the heat. Rita has stoked the wood-fired cook stove and bacon is frying in the black cast iron pan. She hopes the smell will wake Joe. Little Joe left early, before the sun was up to help Mr. McDowell. He carried with him a couple of cold ham biscuits, but Rita knew Mr. McDowell would feed him well at dinner. Mr. McDowell is a good man, smiles Rita, remembering his handsome face when he was a young man.

Music drifts into the kitchen from the radio in Lillian's room. They're up to something, Rita thinks. She'd seen them tip-toeing down the hall, barefooted, too quiet. And now, the radio is louder and the girls are giggling and laughing, a sound heard throughout the small house.

Lillian and Pearl smell the bacon and the coffee but they are busy playing dress up. Early this morning, they raided the closets and chests and wardrobes and carried armloads of dresses, blouses, stockings, bras, corsets, and hats into Lillian's room.

Lillian has a long black skirt on, her widowed great-grandmother's, but she doesn't know that. She stuffs somebody's old fashioned and very large bra with socks before pulling a sweater over her head. Her lumpy chest makes both girls laugh loudly, hysteria nearly taking over. They turn the radio up and dance and wiggle while putting on red, very red, lipstick and powdering their faces.

A favorite song comes on the radio and they turn it up even louder, singing, having so much fun, too much fun for Joe, who, suffering from a hangover, bursts through the door.

"You girls need to…"

He stops and stares at Lillian's enlarged and lumpy bosom and her garishly painted face.

"What the hell are you doing?"

Pearl is embarrassed and ashamed by the look in Joe's eyes. She lowers her head and stares at the floor but Lillian fights back.

"We're putting on a talent show for you and Mama."

"The hell you are. You ain't doing nothing but getting that crap off your face."

Joe is so very angry, his face boiling. He shoves his finger at Lillian's stubbornly set face.

"I ain't telling you again, young lady. Quit your silly pretending and do something useful around here. Everyone pulls their weight but you."

He grabs her by the arm and shakes her roughly. Lillian glares at him.

"You need to grow up. You hear me? Get yourself cleaned up and go in there and help your Mama. You got five minutes. And you, Pearl, got five minutes to get home."

He turns around and slams the door.

Pearl, crying now, puts her arms around Lillian who is stone-faced and still.

"I'm so sorry, Lillian."

"I ain't. I hate him."

Joe storms into the kitchen, head pounding and still angry and his anger grows with each step. He grabs a startled and unprepared Rita by the arm.

"I'm telling you. You don't do something with that girl, I will. You hear me? You understand what I'm saying?"

"I hear you, honey. Yes, I'll do something. Don't you worry. I'll do something today. Just sit down right here and have some coffee. I got bacon and I'll cook you some eggs, over easy, just the way you like them."

Rita rubs his temples in small, firm circles hoping to settle him down

"Let me get you some aspirin. It'll help with the headache."

Joe's anger is now on simmer and he pulls out the chair and sits down heavily. Rita brings him two aspirin and pours a cup of coffee for him. She pulls out a cane-bottomed chair, sits, and arranges her plain blue dress, nervous, but better now that Joe is sitting down. Her fingers pick at Mema's well-worn apron and she talks from nervousness and anxiety.

"Little Joe left early this morning, before the roosters started crowing! All ready to work, he couldn't wait to get started. I'm just so proud of him, I feel like I'm going to bust. Why he'll be out of high school before we know it."

Joe looks straight ahead sipping his coffee. His head hurts and he is tired and he doesn't want to hear Rita's chatter.

"Ain't you got something else to do?"

Rita feels like she is on a thin line between soothing Joe and soothing her pride. Why, oh, why can't life be easy. Why must there always be these choices? She straightens her back and holds her head high. Pride is winning.

"Why, yes, Joe. I always have something to do."

She stands, shaking with nerves and anger and walks out of the kitchen. Lillian, face faded with the rubbed-off makeup, runs to her mama and throws her arms around her waist.

"Oh, Mama. We just wanted to sing for you."

Rita rubs her tangled hair.

"It's all right, baby."

She takes Lillian's hand and walks her outside into the bright sunlight, the cleansing sunlight, the sunlight that bleaches the dirtiest things and leads her to the sunny side of the gnarled cedar tree at the edge of the lawn, out of Joe's sight and out of his hearing. She looks into those green eyes trying so hard not to cry and her heart aches.

"Your daddy loves you, sweetheart. He just doesn't know how to show it. He worries for you, afraid that life will be too hard for you if you have it too easy now. Do you understand?"

Lillian backs away from Rita, stubborn written on her face and in her posture.

"No! I don't understand. He's mean. Mean, mean, mean. And hateful. I wish he weren't my daddy! I wish he'd go away and never come back."

Without hesitating, Rita slaps Lillian in the face. She is surprised at this instantaneous defense of Joe and immediately regrets it, but the words she doesn't want to say come out anyway.

"That is no way to talk, young lady. Shame on you. He works hard everyday to put food on the table and clothes on your back and he never complains. He deserves respect for that."

Oh, when did I learn to lie so well? Rita loses her edge. But I'm not lying, he does work hard. But he is mean, so mean. My little girl is right, always right, and she is so young, so innocent. Oh, God. Help me. Please. She puts her hands over her face and cries.

Lillian feels the sting of her mother's words more than the sting on her face and she feels betrayed, trapped and caught in the nasty adult world. She runs, fast, fast as her strong, sturdy legs can run, away to anywhere that's not here, anywhere that's not red. She runs until she is exhausted but she can't outrun the red dirt that seems to run on forever, as far as she can see, as far as she has ever been. She collapses in the rough red dirt field, scraping her knees bloody but she doesn't care, doesn't even notice. She grabs a handful of dirt and rocks and throws it at nothing.

"You ain't beatin' me!"

Screaming, she grabs another handful of dirt and then another and another. A shower of red dirt flying and falling.

"Ain't, Ain't, Ain't."

Then she stands up, straight and tall, head high, like her Mama and all those other Mamas with green eyes.

"You AIN'T beatin' me!"

############### CHAPTER 4 ###############

The School Play

The kitchen is warm and cozy with the heat from the wood cook stove and the sweet aroma of a baking vanilla cake permeating every nook and cranny. Rita is poised and neat on the outside with a freshly ironed apron over a once stylish cotton dress and, of course, the comforting soft yellow sweater Mema knitted for her so long ago, but the way she is mopping the floor, over and over and over in the same spot betrays her appearance. She just can't get things clean enough, no matter how hard she tries, so she mops and mops and mops.

I miss my Mama, thinks Rita. She was always so sweet and everything was always so clean and so fresh and I was so happy. She wrings the mop into the sink and lowers it into the bucket of soapy water again. I miss Mema. Oh my Mema, how she loved me. What has happened to this world? Why can't I get this house clean? She wrings the mop into the sink again and glances out the window. The hot kitchen air has fogged the glass so she takes the sleeve of her sweater and wipes a circle and there she sees just a bit of Lillian sitting on the cold ground behind the old cedar tree.

"What in the world is that child doing?"

She knocks on the window but gets no response.

Lillian, bundled in Little Joe's old brown coat, sits cross-legged under the tree, Gideon's head on her lap, lost in the pleasure of Lillian's caressing. It's December and the cold has finally set in, but she and Gideon don't care. She hopes it snows, like they say it will, but it never does. Winter is always cloudy and rainy and sometimes icy, but never, ever blinding white and snowy. She leans down to Gideon and whispers.

"One day we'll see the snow. I promise."

Gideon stretches and snuggles his head deeper into her warm lap.

She pulls a piece of crumpled and well-folded paper from the coat's pocket. It is the lines for the school play that she has a part in. It's true that almost everyone in the school has a role to play, but hers has lines. Not many, but enough to make her happy and just enough to make her feel like she is on her way to becoming an actress, a real actress, a Hollywood actress. It is her twelve-year old ticket out of town. Her future.

The play is about the four seasons and Lillian's role is Winter. She reads the lines out loud, testing her voice and her presentation.

"Jack Frost is here to stay, he's nipping at my nose. His icy fingers chill my hands and freeze my little toes."

Well, ain't that the truth!" She says to Gideon.

"I see they haven't changed the winter play."

Rita surprises Lillian who quickly hides the paper under the coat.

"What are you talking about?"

"You know very well what I am talking about, Lillian Dunn. I had that very same role when I was your age. I'll never forget how nervous I was standing up there in front of all those people, especially Mama and Daddy. I was so afraid I would disappoint them."

"I don't need to worry about that now, do I, cause you ain't coming are you?"

The venom in Lillian's words stings.

"Honey, you know I want to."

"Well just do it then. You don't gotta do EVERYTHING he says."

Rita looks down, embarrassed by the truth.

"He don't even know about it, does he? I ain't told him and I don't reckon you have, either."

"Sweetheart, he doesn't approve of girls displaying themselves. It doesn't matter it's only a school play. He thinks it's wrong. That's just the way he is and there is no changing him."

Lillian pulls the paper out from under the coat and hugs Gideon for moral support.

"Well, so he knows, I'm spending Friday night at Pearl's. I'm sure Aunt Helen would like to see you. Without him."

Rita stares at her daughter, perplexed at her complexity. How clever she is, how bold, to tell me her lie. How sweet to think of me. Maybe I should go. My Mama would. She did. But so did Daddy.

"Jack Frost is here to stay…".

Lillian projects her line with confidence.

Rita joins in, remembering the words as if they were from this morning, all those years in between gone and she is Lillian's age again, practicing with her own Mama.

"He's nipping at my nose,"

Lillian looks up at Rita, hopeful and longing for her support.

"His icy fingers chill my hands and freeze my little toes."

Rita claps her hands.

"Well done!"

She holds her hand out to Lillian.

"Let's go in, honey. I've got a cake baking. I'm sure it's about done and you can help me ice it. We can lick the beaters, like we used to…when you were a little girl."

Lillian accepts the peace offering her mother is giving her. She hopes Rita will come to the play but she knows she won't. At least she wants to, that's something, ain't it? She laughs out loud, thinking of her mother as a girl, like her, in a play, like hers. Prim and proper Mama. Quiet Mama. The good girl, she is sure, always a good girl, and not like her after all.

Friday night has arrived and the small, old fashioned school auditorium is packed with the families of the children in the play. Mamas and daddies, aunts and uncles, memas and pawpaws, even the childless have come to witness this annual event they themselves once participated in.

Despite the cold outside, the auditorium is hot and nowhere is hotter than the wings where the children wait for their turn in the spotlight. The smell of chalk dust, old shoes, mildew, and that musk which is particular to humans spreads throughout the air but no one seems to notice. It is a comfortable smell, homey to the costumed children, and it puts them at ease. They are excited and chatty, some practicing their parts, others telling tales on each other. Mrs. McAllister, Lillian's music teacher, and Rita's, so long ago, herds the children into order and with a practiced steady and stern gaze, quiets them.

Lillian, wearing a long white robe has spirals of white construction paper on her head. She is visibly nervous and agitated. She can't be still, swaying from foot to foot, biting her fingernails, pulling at the fair hair in her eyebrows. Pearl, calm as ever and just as smooth as a glass of good whiskey, grabs Lillian's hand and pulls it to her chest. She smiles at her, kisses her cheek and squeezes that hand, gently, but firmly.

"It won't be long, now. I'm so nervous, " she lies, "I wish I was as good as you are."

Lillian looks at her best, best friend, thankful in every way possible for her love and confidence, but it's just not enough to calm her nerves. She hugs Pearl and doesn't want to let go, but Mrs. McAllister is tapping her on the shoulder and whispering.

"You're next, Lillian. Move on up to your mark. And don't forget…project loudly!"

Lillian straightens her back and walks proudly to her mark on the stage. She is not prepared for how bright the lights are, how hot they are, and how dark the auditorium is beyond the lights. She forgets she is an actress and she strains to see if Mama is there, shielding her eyes from the lights with her hand but she can't see past them. Of a sudden, she is acutely aware of being in a spotlight, of everyone looking at her, judging her and she is helpless to defend herself. She is not an actress, after all, just a scared girl, wishing for a moment that she had listened to her Daddy.

She forgets her lines. She forgets everything.

Mrs. McAllister stands on the edge of the stage whispering her name, trying to get her attention, but Lillian is dumbstruck. The teacher sends the group of "Winter" children out and they run, jubilant, around Lillian, throwing white confetti as pretend snow. Lillian glances to the side wing and sees Pearl, nodding her head, mouthing, "go on". Mrs. McAllister catches her eye, and in a bit of rare frustration, points her finger and waves it frantically in a circle. Lillian looks back into the lights and, stuttering, tries to deliver her lines.

"Ja, Ja, Ja,"

She flattens her mouth into a hard, straight line, determined to get it right.

"Jack Frost is here to stay."

She glances at Pearl who is smiling and still nodding her head.

"He's knocking, oh, uh, He's nipping at my, at my nose,"

In the audience, Little Joe sits in the back, the two seats beside him empty. His heart aches for his little sister, for his bold, sassy, and brave little sister, who now stands alone, trying so hard to prove to her world that she has worth. He wills her to remember the lines and whispers them with her, hoping, no, praying that she can hear him.

"His…icy fingers… chill my hands…"

Lillian looks again at Mrs. McAllister who points to her toes and with a sigh of relief, she finishes her role, this last line delivered with confidence.

"And freezes my little toes."

The audience claps politely, but Little Joe stands up and gives a shrill whistle, clapping loudly, hands above his head. Lillian hears the whistle and knows it is him. Finally, she relaxes and smiles, then bows to the audience before skipping off the stage.

Pearl grabs her hand again.

"You did it, Lillian! You're on your way!"

And Lillian believes her. She has forgotten her struggle, her fear and anxiety and remembers only the whistle and the clapping audience at the end. Yes. She is on her way and nothing will stop her now.

Book 2

############### CHAPTER 5 ###############

The Unimaginable

1966

In the late spring, the red dirt fields are covered in the large leaves of the newly transplanted tobacco plants. The ditches are grass green with clumps of He-Loves-Me-Loves-Me-Not daisies and Queen Anne's Lace scattered throughout. Blackberry brambles line the edges of the woods. The thick canes with sharp thorns and green berries give the promise of the cobblers and preserves soon to come. Like everywhere, hopes run high with the prospect of warm weather: a good tobacco crop, an old love renewed, a perfect June wedding, maybe even a new job.

For Lillian, tall and slender now, ponytailed hair and rolled up jeans, it offers another chance for her to believe she can escape her life. And she is more focused than ever on the upcoming high school play. She is sixteen, but her desire to become a Hollywood actress has not diminished, only increased over time. Marilyn Monroe is still her idol, who and what she wants to be, and she can't get there fast enough. She believes, with all her heart, that she will succeed if she gets a part in that play. It's true that Marilyn's end was an unhappy one, but that doesn't matter to Lillian. Norma Jean was a girl, like her, who escaped from an unhappy and unwanted life.

The old house is the same, the floor boards of the porch display a little more rot and the bare wood of the house shows where the paint is now gone, but it's still whole and standing. A porch swing hangs on the side, a gift grudgingly given to Rita by Joe when Little Joe left and joined the army. Lillian drapes across the swing, a well-used paperback in her hands, her foot pushing off a sprawling Gideon, rocking the swing to the gentle rhythm of the song Pearl is slowly strumming on Little Joe's Gibson guitar. News of the war in Vietnam filters through the open window on the porch but the girls aren't paying attention. They are focused on the right here, right now things that occupy them. Lillian lays the book face down on her chest.

Try one: "Romeo, Romeo, where for art thou?" This try is dry and stiff, like she is struggling to remember.

Try two: "Romeo, Romeo, where for art thou?" This try sounds like her daddy calling Gideon. She's not really sure how it should sound.

Try three: "Romeo, Rom…"

Pearl interrupts her attempts.

"Maybe you should think about it like this. She loves him and her heart is pining and yearning for him and at the same time wondering why, oh, why did he have to be from the wrong family."

Pearl strums the sadness out of the sweet old guitar, hoping to give inspiration to her cousin.

"Like this, you see, like this. Listen now."

Lillian listens to the plaintive melody and for a moment, just a swift and fleeting moment, she feels the ache in Juliet's heart, but she can't keep it there. It's gone before she opens her mouth and the words come out empty.

"Romeo, Romeo, where for art thou?"

She knows how barren the words are and, frustrated, throws the book onto the porch and sits up.

"Why don't they just speak English like everyone else?"

Pearl studies Lillian, quietly, thoughtfully, wondering why she is so anxious.

"Does Uncle Joe know you are trying out?"

"I don't know and I don't care. I don't see why he thinks it so wrong, and I don't see why he thinks it's a just a waste of time. What's he know, anyway?"

If only Lillian could harvest this passion. If only she knew she could.

"He thinks all women are good for is getting married and having babies."

She stands up, getting her anger up with her.

"Well, I got news for him. I ain't getting married, ain't having no babies, and I ain't staying here."

"LILLIAN!"

Both girls look down the long driveway to where Lillian's name was called. Rita is running up the river rock road, holding her apron and dress down with one hand and waving a letter high in the air with the other.

"LILLIAN!"

Pearl takes Lillian's hand and gives it a gentle squeeze. Rita, all her breath spent, grabs the porch column and hands the letter to Lillian.

"It's from Little Joe. I can't read it, honey, you do it."

She smooths her apron and sits on the ancient straight-back chair Pearl was sitting on, trying to catch her breath and regain her poise. Lillian rips open the letter and reads out loud.

"Dear Mama, Daddy, Lillian and …"

She glances at Pearl and smiles.

"…Pearl, cause I know you are there with Lil Sis. I'm sorry I have not written sooner but I have been too tired to pick up a pencil. I never knew a human body could march so much and it sometimes seems like that is all we do. I reckon I have it better than some of the boys, though, and am thankful for that. I got my orders today. I am being sent to Vietnam."

Lillian drops the hand holding the letter to her side and looks at her mother who lets out a moan and covers her mouth with her quivering fingers.

"Oh, my poor boy."

Pearl walks to Rita's chair and puts a hand on her shoulder, standing close, knowing how hard it is for her aunt to hear those words.

Lillian is numb. So happy her brother has escaped but now horrified about what he has escaped to. The joy of receiving the letter is gone for all three and in its place are sorrow, fear, and uncertainty. Lillian brings the letter back up and continues, reading methodically.

"Now, y'all do not need to worry for me as I have been trained good and so have all my fellow soldiers. I am proud to do this for my country, and I want to make all of y'all back home proud of me."

Lillian pauses while Rita wipes her eyes with the corner of her apron. She wants to cry, too, but she can't. She feels like she is in a dream world and not the real world at all. Nothing is as it seems.

"Lillian, I want you to take good care of my Indian. Take her out for a spin as soon as Daddy lets you. Keep her covered and clean for me, please. I will send you my new address as soon as I know it. I love you all, Little Joe."

Lillian continues to scan the letter.

"P.S. I am enclosing a new song for Pearl. One of the boys was kind enough to write it out after I showed him her picture."

Lillian hands the second page to Pearl, who clutches it tightly to her heart. They stand there in silence, no one knowing what to say and even if they did, they wouldn't want to break the solemn gravity of the moment so they become lost in it.

A horn blaring from the driveway disrupts the quiet women. A shiny, brand new 1966 growling GTO pulls up to the side of the house and Riley Reynolds steps out. He is a handsome young man. His just so slicked back hair, stylish clothes and spit-polished shoes lets all the world know that he knows he is good looking. He has a charming and disarming smile that at once makes Lillian at ease and on guard. He walks, no swaggers is more like it, to the porch and addresses Rita.

"How you doing, Mrs. Dunn?"

He nods to Pearl out of politeness.

"Pearl."

"I'm doing just fine, Riley. Why don't you come on up and visit for a while. Don't you want to stay and have dinner with us?"

Lillian rolls her eyes at her mother and hands the letter to her. Riley leans his finely dressed body against the dusty porch column.

"No ma'am. Thank you, anyway. I just came by to see if Lillian wanted to go for a ride in my new car."

He glances at Pearl.

"You, too, Pearl."

But it is obvious his heart is not in the invitation.

Lillian doesn't want to look at Riley so she looks at the car instead. He's so good looking she's embarrassed by the thought of the flush that will cover her face if she looks at those pretty eyes and that oh-so-kissable mouth.

"She's a pretty car, all right. I bet she's fast, too".

Just like you, thinks Lillian.

Rita can feel the tension rising off her daughter but she likes Riley and nothing would make her happier right now than to see Lillian paired with a promising young man. Maybe give her all those grand babies she wants. She stands up, smooths her apron and walks to the screen door, giving the kids their privacy.

"You girls go on. Dinner won't be ready for another hour."

Pearl puts the guitar in the case and quickly follows Rita, smiling slyly at Lillian as she makes her escape. She likes Riley, too, for her cousin.

"I think I'll stay here and help Aunt Rita."

The screen door has shut before Lillian has a chance to respond. She's irritated at her family, especially Pearl, but kind of glad at the same time.

"I need to help Mama, too."

Riley steps onto the porch, closer to her.

"You gotta problem with me?"

"No".

Lillian backs up a bit, but Riley steps even closer.

"You gotta a problem with my car?"

"No."

She stands her ground as Riley steps even closer. He leans into her ear and speaks softly. The nearness of him and the warmth of his breath on neck makes her shiver and the shiver embarrasses her, flushing every bit of her face beet red.

"I'll take you to the Dairy-O and buy you a milkshake."

Lillian laughs and pushes him away playfully.

"I ain't that cheap! If it'll make you leave me alone, come on, then, and give me a ride."

She runs to the car, opens the door and hops in.

"Well, ain't you coming?"

Inside, Rita is standing at the kitchen sink, washing potatoes and looking out the window as Riley drives off with her daughter. Oh how I wish she'd just like that young man back, she thinks.

"He seems like such a nice young man."

Pearl, peeling potatoes at the kitchen table, responds.

"Hmmm."

"Do you think he likes her?"

"Oh, yes. I do. I know he does."

Rita turns away from the window, wipes her wet hands on her apron, and looks at Pearl, earnest in her questioning.

"Do you think she likes him?" Please say yes, she thinks.

"I don't know, Aunt Rita. I think she likes him but she doesn't want to."

Rita pulls a chair out from the table and sits down beside Pearl, close enough so that their knees touch.

"Well, that is a strange thing to say. Why do you think that?"

Pearl can't look at Rita. How can her own mother not know what Lillian wants? She's not shy about it, but then, maybe she is shy around Rita, given Uncle Joe's ways and all.

"Lillian doesn't want a boyfriend. She thinks she'll be stuck here for the rest of her life if she gets one. You know, Aunt Rita. She wants to be an actress. Go to Hollywood and be somebody. She's going to be famous and when she is, she's going to move us all there to be with her. It's what she's always wanted."

Rita listens carefully, hearing for the first time, the sincerity of her daughter's desire.

"I see. And do you think this will happen?"

"Not if she starts dating Riley."

Rita closes her eyes. Please let my little girl grow up, here, with me, where she should be. Please, Riley, love my little girl and make her stay. Don't leave me here, alone, with him.

Lillian sits as close to the door of the GTO as she can get, as far away from Riley as she can get. She turns on the radio and finding a country song she likes, puts her dusty bare feet on the dashboard and leans against the window staring at tobacco fields flying past her. She imagines herself on her way to California in this fancy, fast new car. On her way to a new life.

Riley stretches over and gives her arm a nudge.

"Hey. You know. You could sit over here a little closer to me."

Lillian rolls her eyes and continues looking out the window, picturing palm trees in place of oak trees, blue, blue water instead of red dirt fields.

"This sure is a nice car."

"I won't bite. I promise."

"Is it really yours?"

"Sure it is! Come on. Just move over six inches."

He pats the seat where he wants her to move.

"Right here."

Lillian ignores him.

"How'd a boy like you get a car like this?"

If she had this car, she'd be gone, long gone, but it's hard to imagine she'd ever get a car like this, here, in this dirty red place of old fields, old houses, old clothes and old people.

"Move over here just a little bit and I'll tell you."

Lillian moves just a bit closer just to shut him up and Riley smiles that smile that makes charm ooze out of him and onto her.

"I bought it."

"No! You're a smooth liar, Riley."

"I did! I work at the dealership. Open that glove compartment."

She opens it and finds a stack of manila colored business cards.

"Read one of them cards."

She picks up the top one and reads out loud.

"Riley E. Reynolds, Salesman."

"See."

"Well, that's real nice. But what I want to know is, where's Cora Lee? She's your girlfriend, ain't she?"

"Not any more. We broke up."

"Shooo-wee! You sure go through the girls."

"Just looking for the right one, honey."

"Well, why you picking on me?"

Riley flashes her that smile again.

"I ain't picking on you. I like you. You got spunk."

Laughing now, Lillian turns up the radio. Yes, she thinks, I do. That's exactly what I have. And you are the first person to recognize it and I think I like you.

"See that pick-up there? Think you can pass it?"

"Sure, why?"

She gets up on her feet in a crouching position, facing Riley.

"What are you doing?"

"Step on it!"

Riley floors the gas pedal and the muscle car quickly approaches the lumbering pick-up. Lillian pulls down her pants and, with perfect timing, moons the occupants of the truck.

"If I can't go to the moon, I might as well shoot it! Yee-Haw!"

Riley watches with a combination of admiration and disbelief.

"YEAH!"

Inside the truck, Joe, Lillian's father, and his co-worker, Bill, look at the window of the GTO flying past them and see Lillian's bare butt flashing them.

"What was that?" Bill mutters, not sure of what he saw.

"That was a butt. Looked like a girl's butt, too."

Bill laughs.

"Maybe it was an invitation, Joe."

"I could use a butt like that now. What'd you say we go on over to Selma's for a while."

"Sure, whatever. I ain't got nowhere to go fast."

Back in the car, Lillian buttons her pants. She doesn't know that her Daddy was in the truck they passed and right now, she doesn't care. She's feeling good and spunky.

"Man, you are some girl!"

"You think so, huh? Well you just remember this. I'm my own girl. I ain't nobody else's so don't go gettin' no ideas."

Riley pulls the car onto the side of the road and stops it in a cloud of red dust.

"Hey. You just hold on there, honey. I asked you out for a ride in my car. I didn't ask you to marry me."

"Well. I just want you to know the rules. I got one more year of school, and I'm out of here. I can't be distracted."

Riley pats a spot on the seat closer to him.

"Come here."

Lillian relaxes and moves a little toward him.

"Come on. Closer. I never met anyone like you."

He leans in and touches the side of her face.

"I want to kiss you."

"I ain't never kissed a boy before."

"And I ain't never kissed nobody like you."

Lillian lifts her face and Riley gives her a very long and very tender kiss. His mouth is so soft, she thinks, so soft and warm, as she sinks deeper into the kiss. Gone is the school play, for the moment, and gone is the future she imagined for herself, sliding easily to the side, still within reach but harder to pull back with each touch of Riley's lips. Slipping away so slowly, she's not even aware that it is happening.

############### CHAPTER 6 ###############

What we do for Love

It's Thursday and the drama club will soon be posting a list on the bulletin board of those selected to perform the play, Romeo and Juliet. The thrill of Riley's touch still sends shivers down Lillian's spine but so does the chance to be an actress. It seems to Lillian to be a battle for her soul and right now, standing in the hallway waiting for the list to be posted, she thinks the actress will win. After all, she's been that actress for as long as she can remember. Maybe Riley will go with her to California, a thought she has not dared to think to hard about until this moment, and then, she will have everything she wants.

Her musing is interrupted by the clicking of Mrs. Jenkins' heels as she approaches the bulletin board, list in hand. Lillian's heart flips and flops in her chest and she closes her eyes and takes a deep breath, letting it out ever so slowly. Mrs. Jenkins tacks the paper to the board and clicks back down the hallway. Lillian rushes to the list, scrolling down the cast with her index finger. She can't find her name so she tries again, certain that in her hurry, she missed it the first time but again it is not there. Her heart flops to her stomach and she feels dazed and sick, unable for a moment to process what this means. Her name is not on the list, she is sure and she feels like it is the end of the world. Finally, after a lifetime seems to have passed, she turns around and walks down the hall and out of the building.

Riley leans effortlessly against the GTO, waiting for her, hoping she got the part but sure she didn't. Lillian stumbles down the sidewalk, unaware of everything around her. Riley can tell the news is not good.

"Hey, Darlin'. Want a ride?"

Lillian lifts her head and stares at him.

"Sure. Why not."

Riley opens the door for her, ever the gentleman.

"There'll be other plays you know."

Lillian pauses at the open door, dejected and wallowing in self-pity. She wants Riley to comfort her.

"Maybe none for me."

Riley kisses her gently.

"It's gonna be all right. I'll make it all right. I promise. You'll see."

"And just how are you gonna do that? I ain't any good and that's that. Can you please just take me home, now?"

Lillian sits close to the door, arms crossed, wanting nothing more than to be kissing Riley and and not sure why she is so mean to him. He's just being sweet and she is not mad at him, but she is so mad with herself, so very mad with her lost dreams. But, there is the school play in her senior year. So maybe, just maybe, if she practices all summer she will be good enough. Still, even with that little glimmer of hope, Lillian doesn't trust herself to speak and Riley thinks it's best to say nothing, so they ride in silence.

The next morning, just as the sun is beginning to rise, Riley pulls into Lillian's driveway and taps his horn. It's barely light outside and everyone in the house but Rita is still asleep.

"What the hell?" Joe is slowly awakening.

Rita, fully dressed, walks over to the window and pulls back the curtains. It is certainly unusual for such an early morning visitor.

"It's Riley."

She opens the door and calls for Lillian, but she is already running down the hallway and out the door.

"Hey."

Lillian calls out to Riley.

"What are you doing here? Want some breakfast?"

"I want you to go somewhere with me. Come on...get in."

Lillian looks back toward the house. Rita is standing in the doorway, hand on hip, waiting, hoping nothing is wrong.

"How long? I promised Mama I'd help her with the canning."

"I don't know how long. All day, I reckon. Come on. Tell her you'll help her tomorrow. This is special, real special. It's something just for you."

Lillian looks back at Rita, then at irresistible Riley and makes up her mind.

"All right. Let me tell Mama."

It's late morning now and Pearl and Rita pick green beans in the overgrown garden on opposite sides of the row. The sky is cloudless and the sun is hot. Rita wipes the sweat from her brow with her forearm.

"I declare, it seems like these beans grow overnight. I'll be glad when a frost comes and kills them."

She throws a handful into the nearby rusty metal bucket.

"Thank you, Pearl, for helping me."

Pearl smiles.

"It's okay, Aunt Rita. Only I'm sorry I missed Lillian. I haven't see much of her since she started going out with Riley."

The women pick their beans in silence for a few minutes.

"Well, none of us have, honey. Today was a real surprise, though. Riley just showed up early this morning and said he had something to show her. And, she just took off. Didn't matter she was going to help me can these beans. I declare. I just don't know."

Rita is perturbed and starts to pick faster.

"I guess I forget what it was like to be young and in love. I reckon I was the same way. I don't remember much about being young. What about you, Pearl...don't you have a boyfriend?"

Pearl blushes and keeps her eyes on the bean plants.

"Well, sorta."

"Sorta! How can you sorta have a boyfriend?"

"You remember the letter from Little Joe when he sent me the song notes?"

Rita nods.

"He said he showed my picture to the boy?"

Rita nods again.

"I remember."

"Well, we've been writing to each other."

Rita stops picking and stares at Pearl in shock.

"Why Pearl Taylor! Does your Mama know about this? I can't imagine! Why he could be a—"

"It's all right, Aunt Rita. Kevin is Mr. McDowell's nephew! He thinks the sun rises and sets by him and Little Joe does too!"

Rita calms down and smiles when she sees the expression of pure adoration on Pearl's face.

"He sure can write a sweet letter."

"Does he play music, too?"

"He plays everything, fiddle, guitar, banjo. He writes music, too."

"I hope he comes home."

"Me, too, Aunt Rita. Me, too."

The solemnity of this last thought quiets them and they pick in silence to the end of the row. Rita stands and arches her back in a stretch. She notices something on the road in front of the house so she puts her hand over her eyes and squints to see what it is.

"What is it, Aunt Rita?"

"Why, I believe that's Joe's truck."

The old truck is traveling at a good rate of speed and swerving, spewing small rocks and leaving a trail of orange-red dust. Pearl stands up with her bean bucket and looks too.

"Something must be wrong."

Rita smooths her hair and her apron as Gideon bays and bounds toward the truck. Both women run to the back doorstep where they put the bean buckets. Rita hurries to the front side of the house in time to see the truck come sliding in on the river rock drive, barely missing her.

Joe stumbles out of the truck with a brown paper bag in his hand. It is wrapped around a canning jar of moonshine which he holds by the neck. He sees Rita but not Pearl who stands off by the side of the house.

"What the hell you looking at? You look like you seen a ghost."

He sniggers as he walks toward Rita and puts his face in hers, eyes bugged.

"I'm back!"

Rita reaches out to him, touching his arm gently.

"Come on, honey. Let's go inside."

She tries to put her arms around him, but he roughly pushes her away.

"Get away from me you damn ole' bitch."

He reels from pushing her and falls to the ground still holding his liquor jar not spilling even a drop. Rita rushes to his side, moves the jar carefully, so as not to spill any as she struggles to get him to his feet.

"Pearl, come help me!"

Poor, shy Pearl does not want to go any where near Joe. She doesn't like him and never has. Her own daddy is kind and soft-spoken and has never been out right mean. She doesn't know why, but Joe makes her feel like she is a bad girl and she knows she isn't, but it makes her uncomfortable anyway.

"Come on, now. I can't do this without help."

Pearl gives in to Rita's pleading and together they get a barely conscious Joe into the house. They manage to drag him to the sofa and Pearl quickly retreats to the kitchen door, watching as Rita ministers to him, wiping his face with the corner of her apron.

"Oh, Joe. What has happened?"

Without removing her attention to her husband, Rita speaks softly to Pearl.

"Pearl. Bring me a pot."

Pearl disappears and returns with a small, deeply dented aluminum pot. She rushes back to the protection of the kitchen doorway. Joe moans and Rita rolls him onto his side facing the pot where he throws up the rough, raw liquor. Pearl goes into the kitchen and returns with a small bowl, a wet rag and a glass of water. She gives them to Rita and scurries back to the doorway.

Rita wrings the rag and gently wipes Joe's face. He rouses, leans up on his elbow, and roughly takes the water she offers him to drink. His eyes are heavy-lidded and bloodshot, his face pale, punctuating the deep furrows lining it, making them feel even deeper, making him look even older. One greasy lock of graying hair falls over his face.

"Where's my liquor?"

He sits up, his hands shaking slightly, as Rita stands.

"It's all right, Joe. It's outside where you left it."

Her eyes do not leave his.

"Pearl? Please get Joe's liquor."

Pearl, grateful for the escape, silently slips out the kitchen door. Rita leans toward Joe and speaks softly to him, trying to soothe him and find out what has happened.

"Everything's okay, Joe. Pearl'll get the jar."

Joe rubs his hands on his face. He props his head in his hands, his eyes bleary and dull. He is so tired of fighting life, but he doesn't know any other way to be. He can't figure out why he is so mean to Rita. She's the only one who understands him, who pacifiers him, who makes him feel calm.

"I don't want the jar. I want some coffee. Can you fix me some coffee, Mama?"

Rita's body sags with relief.

"Sure I can, honey. You wait right here."

Rita walks calmly into the kitchen and over to the window. She motions for Pearl, still standing in the doorway, to sit down. Holding the jar, Pearl slinks into the living room's nearest chair and tries to be invisible. She and Joe sit there is silence for a few moments, Pearl looking anywhere but at Joe and Joe looking only at her. Finally, her eyes are drawn to his.

"What you looking at?" Joe growls.

"I'm looking at you, Uncle Joe."

"Well, don't!"

They lock eyes until Rita comes in with the coffee and he releases his gaze. He has never liked Pearl's daddy so he can't like her either, so he believes.

"Here you go, honey."

Rita hands him the cup and sits at his feet, patiently waiting for an explanation. Joe sips, radiating sullenness and meanness. He looks only at his coffee cup when he finally speaks.

"I got fired this morning."

Rita sits up on her knees and grabs Joe's legs.

"Oh, Joe! What did you do?"

He slaps at her hands and pushes her away. She falters slightly but regains her balance and her poise.

"I went to work everyday for twenty damn years. That's what I did."

He waves one finger in the air angrily.

"Never laid out once. Those God damn sons of bitches."

Rita is confused. Farm life she understands but not factory life.

"But I don't understand."

"If the company ain't making money, then I can't work. That's it. That's what they told me."

"But what will we do?"

Rita looks intently at Joe, then smooths her apron and looks away. How can they live without his salary? How can life change so fast? What will happen to us?

"Maybe I can take in ironing. I don't mind doing that."

Joe hands Rita the coffee cup and stands up.

"I'm going to lay down. I'll figure something out later."

He looks at Pearl.

"Maybe I'll go see my brother-in-law."

Joe stumbles down the hallway and into the bedroom. Rita sits on the sofa, stunned, starring at the blank tv screen. Pearl, unnoticed, sits in the chair watching her. She's never seen anyone as mean as Uncle Joe. She feels bad that she didn't understand what Lillian's life was really like. And Aunt Rita, poor, poor Aunt Rita. Does her mother know about Uncle Joe? Should she tell her? What will happen to these people who she loves so much? All she can do is say a small prayer.

"Please, God. Be with Aunt Rita today."

Over one hundred miles away, Lillian and Riley sit outside at a colorful beachside diner eating burgers and fries and drinking Pepsi Colas. The sun shines brightly, not a cloud in the sky, and a warm, gentle breeze floats by them. Lillian has never been happier. There's no red dirt anywhere, just white sand and rough green grass that grows even in the cracks of the sidewalks.

"I can't believe we've driven all the way here! What made you think of this?"

"You're always talking about getting out of town. I thought I'd like to make that dream come true. You know, Like Queen for a Day… or…"

He grabs a duffel bag beside him, unzips it and pulls out an old 8mm home movie camera.

"Movie star for a Day!"

"Where'd you get that?"

"Pawn shop"

Lillian can't believe that Riley can be so thoughtful. That anybody would think about her so. She wipes her wet eyes and face with her hand.

"Why do you have to be so nice to me?"

"I like you, darlin'. I'm going make your dreams comes true at least for today. Finish up those fries so we can get to the beach. I can't wait for you to see the ocean."

Lillian leans over the table and kisses him.

The sea oats seem to float on the large sand dunes that lead to the ocean, waving rhythmically, to and fro. There are no people, no houses, nothing but the dunes as far as the eye can see. Riley runs ahead of Lillian and films as she walks over the sand dune and sees the ocean for the first time. She puts her hand over her mouth and gasps.

"It's so beautiful... I've never imagined anything so...big. So...empty."

Riley laughs and takes her hand.

"Come on, let's go down to the water."

"No...you go. I want to sit here and look at it for a little bit. Let me just do that, okay?"

A flock of seagulls swoop over her head and one flies almost close enough for her to touch.

"Oh my gosh! Look at them! Get their picture, too, Riley. Oh, if only I had wings."

Lillian sits down in the sand, crossing her legs, closing her eyes and facing the ocean. She takes a deep breath and opens her eyes again. Riley sits beside her and pulls a joint out of his pocket, lights it, and takes a toke. Lillian sniffs at the smoke.

"What kind of cigarette is that?"

"It's a joint. Like a cigarette only better. You smoke it like this..."

Riley inhales deeply, holds his breath and slowly lets out the smoke.

"Let me try it."

Lillian imitates Riley and they finish smoking the joint in silence, watching the ocean, Lillian in an even greater sense of wonder and contentment. When they finish smoking, Riley removes his shoes and rolls up his pants, then tugs at Lillian's leg so he can take off her shoe.

"What are you doing with my leg?"

"Don't you want to walk in the water?"

"No. I want to kiss you, then I want to take a nap."

She closes her eyes and puckers so Riley kisses her gently and she opens her eyes.

"I reckon I really like you, too, you know."

The sun has gone down and it is full dark when Lillian and Riley return home. From inside the house, Joe watches them kiss at the foot of the porch stairs. They are in a very close and sensual embrace, still, quiet, and slow, reluctant to let each other go. It has been a perfect day for Lillian and she doesn't want it to end.

Pearl stands in the background and watches Joe close the curtain. He mutters curses and retreats to his bedroom only to return a moment later with a shotgun. Pearl quietly slips into the kitchen, picks up the phone, and dials the operator, keeping a close watch on the front door.

Lillian and Riley are lost in each other. When the kiss ends, she lays her head on Riley's chest and he strokes her hair.

"Thank you for my day, honey. I'll remember it forever. It's the best day I ever had."

Riley kisses the top of her head. At that moment, Joe appears at the edge of the porch firing the shotgun into the sky. Riley and Lillian, startled, look up at him in shocked disbelief. Rita stands in the open doorway screaming, Pearl's arms around her.

"No! Joe!"

Riley jumps in front of Lillian.

"What the...?"

"Daddy!"

Joe points the gun at Riley, his arm shaking from the effects of drinking.

"Get the hell off my land."

Rita tries to take Joe's arm, but he shrugs her off roughly. For added emphasis, he fires the gun again. Lillian and Rita both scream. Riley backs away when Joe reloads the gun and points it at him.

"You ain't going fast enough, you son of a bitch. Now git!"

He fires the gun just over Riley's head.

"And don't you ever show your face here again."

Riley, terrified, moves faster and Lillian runs after him, pleading in her face. She speaks only loud enough for him to hear.

"I'll see you tomorrow."

Joe points the gun at Lillian.

"You! Girl!"

Lillian and Riley freeze.

"Get your butt up here."

Riley takes her arm and pulls her toward him. The gun fires again. Lillian looks at Riley, begging him to do something but not sure what. Just as he lets her go, the sheriff pulls in, lights flashing, behind Riley's car.

Sheriff McRae is a late middle-aged man, born and raised in the same county and knows just about everyone. He gets out of the car, surveys the scene, nods to Riley and Lillian, then focuses his attention on Joe who has reloaded the gun and has it pointed in the sheriff's direction.

"Well now, Joe. What seems to be the problem?"

Joe, still trembling with anger and confused by liquor, is puzzled by the presence of the sheriff.

"That damn son of a bitch got me fired, and I want him off my land."

Sheriff McRae keeps his eyes on Joe and he walks slowly toward the porch until he comes to the railing at the bottom step. He leans against it and Joe, still confused, lowers the gun. McRae takes out a pack of cigarettes and offers one to Joe who takes it. The sheriff lights both cigarettes. He takes a long drag and exhales slowly before speaking.

"Seem's to me...it's the boy's daddy who works at the factory. Riley here works over at the car lot."

"Yeah, I know that."

Joe thinks for a moment.

"Makes no difference to me, though. I don't want him around me or the girl."

He eyes McRae, not backing down on this point.

"Doesn't seem fair to punish the son because of the father."

"She's my girl and you can't tell me what to do with her."

The sheriff shifts positions and takes a drag off his cigarette.

"You got a point there, Joe. But I can tell you what to do with that gun. Now, I'm not one to bring up the past but I ain't had any trouble out of you for twenty years, and I'd just as soon be able to say that twenty years from now. So put the gun away and leave this here boy alone."

He pauses for emphasis.

"I'm truly sorry for you and your troubles and you know I'll help you any way I can."

He throws the cigarette down and puts it out with his foot. Joe is subdued, remembering old acts and old promises and he lowers his head.

"I'll put the word out that you'll be needing work. I'm sure you'll find a job in the next few days."

Rita takes the shotgun from Joe's hands and leads him into the house. Pearl rushes to the sheriff and throws her arms around him.

"Thank you, Uncle Bud."

He pats his niece on the shoulder.

"Come on. I'll give you a ride home."

Crying, Lillian hugs Riley in defiance of her father. Sheriff McRae's booming voice interrupts the embrace.

"You best get on boy. He ain't a man to be around when he's been drinkin', but I guess you figured that out. Oh. Just so you know. He would have shot you. Killed you if he could."

*************** CHAPTER 7 ***************

A Sad State of Affairs

Lillian pulls the Indian motorcycle out of the worn down shed. Little Joe wants her to take care of it, to ride it, and she figures the time is right. If she is to ever see Riley again, she'll need to leave on wheels. She hops on, starts it easily and takes off, the wind in her hair, wondering if she could ride it all the way to California. How much money would it take to get her there? Maybe she could get a job. For a little while, that's all. Just a little while. Save a bit of money. Take off. Never see Daddy again. But then maybe not Riley, either.

She turns onto River Road, then onto a narrow dirt path with no name that leads her to the river. She parks the Indian beside an ancient wood-sided gray fishing shack and hops off, checking her watch. Riley should be here any minute. Please let him come, she thinks. Don't be scared, she prays as she sits on the bank of the river.

Before long, she hears the GTO coming down the road and she runs to greet Riley, thankful he hasn't changed his mind but scared he might of and is just coming to tell her they can't see each other any more. Riley gets out of the car and she rushes to him, embracing him tightly. He kisses her then peels himself away from her embrace. He nods toward the Indian.

"How'd you manage that?"

"He don't know, of course. He was laid out when I left."

Riley is frightened for Lillian and not at all sure they should be meeting. He takes her by the arms and speaks earnestly to her.

"We need to be careful. YOU need to be careful. He's one mean son of a bitch."

Lillian takes a step backward.

"You're not scared are you? You wanna break up with me? Is that it?"

Riley pulls her to him and starts kissing her again.

"I'm not scared. Don't you worry about that. It's just...I sure have missed you, darlin'."

The sweet kisses become more passionate and his hands begin to grope. Lillian tries to pull away, but Riley holds her tighter.

"Shhh, shhh now."

She relaxes a bit which makes him bolder with his hands.

"Stop it!"

Lillian struggles to escape his embrace and Riley lets her go, putting his hands in the air.

"Okay. Okay. Geez, darlin', I'm just trying to comfort you."

He puts his hand on her face and she leans her head toward his hand wedging it between her face and shoulder. She pleads her case.

"I want you so bad, honey. I lay awake at night and my body hurts from wanting."

She pulls away from him.

"But I want a chance at a life way away from here. I don't want to be stuck here, poor, raising a sorry bunch of red dirt girls like me, hating their world, hating you. That would kill me."

She hugs Riley tightly around the chest.

"Please understand. Please, please, please understand."

Riley puts his arms around her and kisses her head.

"It doesn't have to be that way, darlin'. I've got protection. Do you know what I mean?"

Lillian starts crying and Riley kisses the tears on her face.

"I love you, baby. I'll get you out of here. I promise. I swear I will. We'll finish school then I'll drive you to California, myself"

Riley picks her up and carries her into the fishing shack. Lillian, afraid, excited, aroused, goes willingly, sure that when she comes out, she will never leave, sad and happy at the same time.

The next day, Lillian sways gently on the front porch swing smiling to no one but herself. Pearl strums her guitar and looks at Lillian suspiciously. The faint sounds of the TV and the hiss of Rita's ironing are heard through the open window.

"You look mighty happy today. Did you see Riley?"

"Maybe."

"You did!"

Lillian stops swinging.

"Shhhh!"

She puts her finger on her closed mouth and looks toward the open window. Pearl lowers her voice.

"So did your Daddy scare him off or does he still love you?"

Lillian grins slowly and nods.

"Not scared away, then?"

She shakes her head, grinning in a self-satisfied way. Pearl is irritated with her.

"Well, is he going with you or are you staying here?"

"I'll worry about that next year."

Pearl is ready to respond but is alarmed by a black car coming down the driveway. She stares intently at it and Lillian follows her fixed gaze.

"This is not good! Mama!"

The car gets closer to the house. They see two uniformed men in the front seat.

"Mama! You need to come out here now!"

Rita comes to the screen door, smoothing her apron, perplexed at the intensity of Lillian's voice. Then she sees the car and the two men who get out and walk toward the porch. Pearl and Lillian step on either side of Rita and they join hands sure that in this moment, they need each other.

One man, solemn in his duty, removes his hat and addresses Rita.

"Ma'am. Are you Mrs. Joseph Dunn?"

Rita nods her head.

"I regret to inform you, ma'am, that your son, Private Joseph Martin Dunn has been killed in action in Vietnam."

Rita cries out and slumps, held up by Lillian and Pearl. How can this be, thinks Lillian. How can this be true. Why now, why today, why ever, why him? What do I do? Oh, how can Mama stand this. What will Daddy do? How will life go on? Oh, my brother, my poor brother. Please help me, Lord.

The small church is packed. There is no standing room for the memorial service of the town's favorite son. Lillian stands at the podium while Pearl sits beside her holding Little Joe's guitar.

"I want to thank all of y'all who have said such kind things about my brother, Little Joe. He was the lamp in my life and I don't know how I will get through the rest of it without his light to guide me."

She starts crying, then composes herself, eyes on her father, as she speaks. He is unshaven and grizzled, inconsolable at the loss of his beloved son.

"So please, folks, if you see me stumble, give me a hand and if I fall, help me to get up and…"

She breaks down into uncontrollable sobs and Riley takes her by the arm leading her to a seat in the front row. Pearl stands, places the guitar on the chair, faces the audience and begins to sing. Everyone cries but Joe. His face is blank and his eyes appear soulless.

"When the curtains of night are pulled back by the stars
And the beautiful moon sweeps the sky.
When the dewdrops from heaven are kissed by the rose,
It's there that my memory flies.

> So go where you will,
> On land or on sea,
> I'll share all your sorrows and cares.
> At night as I kneel by bedside to pray,
> I'll remember you, love in my prayers."

When Pearl finishes there is not a dry eye in the church. There is no funeral for Little Joe. His body is somewhere in Vietnam, never to come home to the red dirt he loved so much.

It's been a month since the memorial service for Little Joe. Lillian and Pearl, nervous in their best Sunday dresses with their hats and white gloves, sit in the waiting room of the old, musty law office of Axel Drake. Pearl takes Lillian's hand.

"It'll be all right. Just hold my hand and you'll be okay. I promise."

Lillian gives Pearl a sad smile and a slight squeeze of her hand. The door opens and Mr. Drake, a tall, balding and imposing man, comes into the room. The girls stand.

"Good morning, Pearl."

He reaches out his hand to Pearl's and gives her an old fashioned southern gentleman handshake - a gentle squeeze. He turns to Lillian.

"And you must be Lillian. I'm Axel Drake, Joseph Dunn's legal representative."

He takes her outstretched hand and gives it a squeeze.

"Yes sir. Nice to meet you."

"Now if you girls would be so kind as to step in here."

He gestures toward the room he came out of and leads them through the door. Lillian feels like she has walked onto a movie set and can't help but be awed. It's an antique lawyer's office filled with diplomas, old maps, and old prints. Overflowing bookshelves line the walls. Somehow it is cluttered and neat at the same time.

Axel steps behind his large walnut desk and motions the girls to sit in the two low chairs in front of him.

"Please, have a seat and we'll get started."

Lillian and Pearl sit and lean forward expectantly. Mr. Drake clasps his hands together and begins.

"As I have told you, I was the legal representative of Joseph Dunn and I am now representing his estate."

The girls look at each other with curiosity. Mr. Drake continues.

"Just before Joseph left for Vietnam, he came to me and asked me to draw up a will for him. You girls are the beneficiaries of that will. Now. First. Pearl. It seems Joseph was in possession of a 1933 Sunburst Gibson guitar. He has willed that you take possession of that guitar and that it be yours henceforth. He also wants you to have this."

He hands her a sealed envelope which she takes, perplexed. Mr. Drake picks up a folded piece of official paper and turns to Lillian.

"Now to Lillian. This is the title to Joseph's 1949 Indian Chief motorcycle. In accordance with his will, I have had the title changed to reflect your ownership. This is yours to do with as you please and no one can take it from you. Do you understand what I am saying?"

Lillian wipes the tears from her cheeks and nods her head.

"It was also the will of Joseph that you take sole possession of all the monies he possessed at the time of his death. That amounts to $3,253.86 after I have deducted certain expenses incurred in carrying out his will. I have, at his suggestion, deposited this in a bank account for you with myself as guardian. He also asked me to give you this."

He holds up a sealed envelope then pushes a bankbook and the letter toward the end of the desk. Lillian picks them up. He and the girls stand and he shakes the hand of each one again.

"I wish you both good luck with your new found possessions. By the way, Lillian, I forgot to mention. You can only withdraw money with both of our signatures until you are eighteen. Would you like to withdraw some today?"

Lillian glances at Pearl then back to the attorney and shakes her head.

"No Sir, Mr. Drake. I don't need any money right now."

"Are you sure? Perhaps you'd like a new dress, new shoes maybe? After all, it's not every day a young girl comes into such a sum of money. I'm sure your brother wouldn't mind."

"I don't need any money right now, Sir. Besides, I know why Little Joe wanted me to have that money, and I'm gonna save it until I'm ready."

Mr. Drake puts his hands in the air, giving up.

"All right, then. If you do need any between now and the time you're eighteen, just come on by. Don't worry about an appointment."

Mr. Drake walks to the front of the desk.

"Pearl, give my regards to your parents. And Lillian, here's my card. If you need anything, if there's ever anything I can do for you, call or come see me. My door is always open for you."

Lillian takes the card and puts it in her purse.

"Thank you so much."

He opens the door for the girls and they leave.

"Enjoy that guitar, Pearl!"

"I will, Mr. Drake. Thank you."

CHAPTER 8

The Past

Bud McRae was always a friend to Rita. He knew the true story of Rita and Joe Dunn and he wanted to keep them safe. He knew things were about to get real bad so he had a talk with Mr. Drake.

The diner is old but pristine clean with easy access across from the law office. Mr. Drake and the sheriff sit in the far corner eating homestyle meatloaf with mashed potatoes and green beans. Axel wipes his mouth with his napkin and leans back.

"Well, Bud. I've done all I can do. The offer is made, the cards are on the table. Let's hope she understands."

"I appreciate it, Axel. That ole son-of-a-bitch daddy of hers has been on a week long drunk. Hadn't been back to work since he got news of Little Joe. He's turned out just like his sorry God damn daddy, drinking and whoring. I don't think that poor little gal has got a chance."

Axel leans in.

"Why do you say that? What was his daddy like?"

McRae leans closer to Axel.

"He was found shot to death, floating face down in the river, if that tells you anything."

"Do they know who did it?"

McRae shakes his head and smirks

"The investigation was short and left open."

Axel persists.

"But you know who did it?"

McRae flags down a waitress with a coffee pot.

"Just a little more coffee, honey, and a piece of that apple pie. Thank you, now."

She pours the coffee, and he leans over the table, speaking quietly to Axel.

"Like I was saying, Joe's daddy was as mean and sorry a drunk as there ever was. He wasn't even allowed at Selma's! He beat his wife and kids and most people round here believed he even raped his own daughter."

"His own daughter?"

McRae nods his head slowly and sips on his coffee.

"Joe really loved pretty little Rita Walker and Rita loved Joe, but she didn't like his drinking or his daddy so she started dating Sean McDowell. That was devastating to Joe, who thought Rita was his salvation in life. Well, it so happens that Joe and his daddy were out drinking when they spied Rita and Sean down by the river."

1946

Joe and his dad, a dirty, scrawny bit of a man, sit in the woods near the river passing time and drinking from a canning jar of moonshine. Dad pushes Joe's shoulder and laughs as Joe falls over, giggling at this sudden change of position. Dad cocks his head, thinking he hears something. He grabs Joe and pulls him up close to him, their noses nearly touching.

"Shhh!"

"D' ya hear that?"

Joe thrusts his head forward and listens with wide-eyed exaggeration. A girl's laughter filters through the forest. Dad stands up.

"Shut up, boy, and come on with me."

The men sober up and creep through the woods toward the sound. Joe's dad motions for Joe to be still and he parts the branches of leaves that are in his way. He watches Rita and Sean McDowell, just seventeen, sit at the river's bank, skimming rocks across the water's surface. Sean takes Rita's arm, moving it back and then forward, demonstrating the best skimming stroke. He slides his hand down her arm, enclosing her hand in his.

Joe balls his fist, blaming Sean for taking Rita away from him. The moonshine makes his anger uncontrollable. He is breathing hard, his nostrils flaring with each breath he takes and be begins to tremble as he watches the two teenagers. His dad, sensing his rage, turns and whispers.

"She ain't nothin' but a whore, son. Nothing but a whore."

Sean and Rita are oblivious to the looming presence of the two men. Sean leans down to kiss Rita at the same time that Joe's dad whacks him with a dead tree limb, knocking him into Rita's lap. She looks up and screams.

Sheriff McRae pounds his fist on the table.

"Then good ole dad held down Rita while his son raped her. But dad was not to be outdone by his son. He had his turn as well."

Axel, fork in hand has not moved during this retelling of events.

"So McDowell recovered and shot the dad?"

McRae shakes his head slowly and takes a bite of the hot, steaming pie.

"About a month later, the old man showed up dead. Rita and Joe got married and eight months after that, Little Joe was born."

McRae pauses to sip his coffee and collect his thoughts.

"Joe's done pretty good since then. Trouble with them Dunns though, is they can't take adversity. Ain't got no grit."

"Why didn't McDowell kill Joe?"

Sheriff McRae shrugs. He won't be giving away all his secrets today. He slides a fat envelope toward the attorney who looks at him questioningly.

"Money for the family. People have been dropping off fives and tens, whatever they can afford, here and there."

Axel peers inside the envelope and fans through the money with his fingers.

"Save it for the girl or give it to her aunt. Helen would use it judiciously. If you give it to the family, only the whiskey and the whores will get it.

The afternoon is hot, the sun bright and cheery, assaulting the gloom that hangs over the Dunn house. Lillian and Pearl sit on the front porch, as usual, with Lillian in the swing and Pearl in the straight back chair, leaning against the house. Each holds the letter from Little Joe. As if protecting the girls, Gideon lies at attention on the top step to the porch.

Lillian hugs her letter to her chest.

"You read yours first."

Pearl opens the envelope and removes the letter.

"Dear Sweet Pearl, I know you have always loved my old guitar so I am happy to know that it will be in your hands. Know that whenever you play it, I will be listening, so play it a lot. Love, Little Joe."

Her eyes tear up but she reaches down beside her and picks up the guitar.

"You don't have to read yours now, Lillian."

"Thank you. I don't think I want to read it. I think I'm never going to read it. I already know what it says. It says get out of town Lil Sis. It says, here is your ticket out of her;. a motorcycle and a year's worth of money. Get on the Indian and ride like the wind. Don't look back and don't stop til you get to the moon."

She begins to sob.

"And when you get there, look down on our little house and remember me, who never wanted to leave."

She puts her head in her hands and cries hard.

"I can't believe I'll never see him again."

############### CHAPTER 9 ****************

The High Cost of Moonshine

Joe, dressed in a tee shirt and starched and ironed underwear sits in his chair in the living room watching a game show on TV. He is unshaven and unwashed, his dull eyes red and his face puffy. The moonshine jar in his hand catches a faint ray of light, glistening and beckoning him to take another swallow. He's on pure automatic now, trying desperately to drown his sorrows, but only making his life more miserable.

Rita is in the kitchen preparing dinner and the sounds of cooking can barely be heard over the TV. Still, Joe is aggravated by the noise.

"Shut that racket up in there. I can't hear the TV."

"I'm sorry, honey. I can't cook without making noise."

"Well, come in here and turn the damn TV up then."

He takes another sip of moonshine.

"All right, Joe. I'll be there in a minute."

Joe slams the jar down on the table, picks up his cigarette pack and lighter and straightens up.

"I want you to do it now, Goddamn it. Git in here!"

Rita walks calmly into the room, smoothing her apron. As she crosses over to the TV, Joe throws the pack of cigarettes on the floor. Lillian comes to the doorway, unnoticed by Joe.

"Bend over and pick them cigarettes up for me."

Rita stops and looks at him, puzzled.

"I said, BEND OVER AND PICK UP THE GODDAMN CIGARETTES."

She squats and reaches for the pack.

"All right, Joe."

She picks up the cigarettes and hands them to him, trying hard not to irritate him further.

"I said BEND over, you stupid bitch. Now turn around and bend over."

Rita is afraid of Joe, scared enough to be compliant. She turns her back to him and bends over. Joe looks at her butt and lifts the hem of her skirt with his foot. He tilts his head to peer under her dress.

"You ain't got nothing but a ugly, skinny old ass. It ain't good for nothing. My daddy was right about you."

He takes his foot and boots her to the ground. She stays where she has fallen, not making eye contact with Joe. He stands up rubbing his crotch.

"I'm gonna go get some real ass."

He walks around her and into the bedroom. Rita straightens up, sees Lillian in the doorway, and frantically motions her to leave. Lillian disappears into the kitchen as Rita stands and tries to smooth her apron and hair before following. She is mortified that Lillian witnessed her humiliation but more upset that she had to see her father behaving in such a way. She takes a deep breath and follows her daughter into the kitchen.

Lillian sits at the table, her eyes angry and snappy. Rita sits beside her and takes her hand. Tears begin to stream down her face, but she does not make a sound. They hear the front door slam, followed by the sound of the old truck leaving down the driveway.

"I'm so sorry you had to see that, baby. He's only like that when he's been drinking hard. He really didn't hurt me. Just my pride."

She puts her other hand on top of Lillian's. Lillian turns her head to avoid looking at her. Rita pats her hand, soothing herself more than her daughter.

"Your daddy is a good man. I believe that with all my heart. He's had to fight the curse of that liquor every day of his life for the last twenty years and he's done that for me and you and Little Joe. I know he's suffering and now..."

Finally, Rita breaks down. After a few moments she recovers and uses the corner of her apron to wipe the tears. Lillian sits in stunned silence, cold hearted, but softening.

"Now that Little Joe is gone, he can't...not that he doesn't love you, honey. But he can't see any reason to fight the liquor. And the liquor makes him hate me and you for being the ones to live."

She pauses to catch her breath and her thoughts.

"I want you to leave here, Lillian. You have-"

"No, Mama! Don't say that. I can't leave you here with him."

Rita leans over and puts her hands on Lillian's face.

"Honey, he can't hurt me worse than he's already done, but he can hurt you terribly, terribly bad."

She stands up, automatically smoothing her apron.

"You go pack a few things and go on over to Pearl's, just for a few days. Give him a chance to sober up."

Lillian hugs her Mama and starts to cry.

"Oh, Mama. Why is everything so hard?"

Rita has no answers for her daughter. She doesn't even have answers for herself.

"You best be going, now."

Lillian nods and leaves Rita alone in the kitchen with the half-cooked dinner.

When Rita hears the sound of the motorcycle and is sure Lillian has left, she goes to the closet in the bedroom and pulls out an old shotgun and a box of shells. She loads the gun and takes it to the kitchen where she places it in the corner, behind the mop and the broom.

Slow and determined, she opens the refrigerator, takes out a Pepsi and sits at the table, thinking of the past and gathering her courage once more.

1946

Young Rita lies on the ground struggling, her arms held over her head by Joe. Joe's dad looms over her undoing his pants.

"Hold her good, son. This won't take long."

Joe's face, upside down is the face Rita sees while she is being raped. She ceases to struggle as the pain sears through her body. In a few minutes, Joe's dad rolls off her.

"Your turn, son."

Rita refuses to take her eyes off of Joe's face until he has finished. Joe did not look at her once, his eyes tightly closed.

Thereafter, Rita stalked the riverbank every day with a shotgun. After nearly a month had passed, she found her quarry, on their way to the oblivion moonshine offers. She steps out from behind a tree, shotgun loaded, finger on the trigger. Joe sees her first.

"What the hell?"

Dad stands up, sways for a moment then starts toward her angry that this scrawny girl would dare threaten him or his son.

"Why, it's the whore."

Rita pulls the trigger, without hesitating, and he spins and falls face forward into the river. She swings the gun toward Joe.

"I'm pregnant. It's your baby, or your dad's. Ain't no way of knowing, I reckon."

Joe just stares at her, not sure what to do. For a moment, he is afraid of Rita, of what she might do to him. He wants to take a swig from the jar but the look in Rita's eyes stops him.

"If you stop drinking and promise to marry me, I'll put the shotgun down. For the sake of the baby, you hear me."

Joe hears her now. He quickly throws the jar into the woods.

"I'll quit drinkin', I promise. Won't have another drop. Please don't shoot me. The baby needs his daddy. I can do that for you, you know I can. I love you, Rita."

Rita lowers the gun.

"If you ever hurt me again, I'll track you down like a dog, then I'll lay you in the ground beside your daddy. I promise you that, baby or no baby."

1966

Selma's is a dirty, dank and dimly lit bar where women are easy and can be had for free or for money. Curtained off areas exist for privacy. The bar is lined with hard-core drinkers, Joe and his friend, Bill, among them. A plump and skimpily dressed young woman sits at a small table near the bar smoking, hoping to attract the attention of one of the men.

Selma, the owner and bartender, is middle-aged, faded, old beyond her years, like most people in their town. She opens a beer and hands it to Joe.

"Why don't you go on back home, Joe? Take a nap and come back later. We ain't going nowhere."

He chugs his beer.

"I ain't goin' home 'till I've seen me a good lookin' piece of ass."

The men at the bar laugh. Joe takes another chug of beer and looks at Selma.

"Come on, Selma, turn around and show me your ass."

Bill pipes up.

"Yeah, Selma! Show us your ass."

"Shut up, Bill."

She leans on the bar in front of Joe, displaying her ample and barely covered breasts.

"You ain't man enough to look at my ass."

The room falls silent, the jovial attitude gone. Joe grabs his cigarette pack and lighter.

"Fuck you."

He lights a cigarette and blows the smoke in her face. The plump girl comes over to Joe and rubs on his back.

"Hey, Joe. I'll show you my ass."

"Let me see it, then."

The girl walks a few steps away from Joe, bends slightly at the waist and wiggles her butt.

"That ain't showing us your ass. Get that skirt out of the way!"

The girl lifts her skirt showing a fairly fat bottom with too small underwear. The men hoot in unison. Joe takes his foot and rubs it on the girl's bottom.

"Now that's a nice ass. Too bad it's so fat."

He kicks her like he did Rita, knocking her to the floor. The men stop hooting as the girl whimpers and scrambles to get out of the way. Selma comes from around the bar with a baseball bat in her hand. The men stand back away, giving her room. She pushes the bat at Joe, hard, knocking him off the stool. He stumbles but regains his balance.

"Get out of here you son of a bitch and don't you come back."

The men in the bar move close behind her, ready to assist in case Joe feels inclined to fight. Joe puts his hand out to get his cigarettes and Selma slams the bat across his shoulder. He hollers and looks at her in disbelief.

"That's for actin' like your Goddamn daddy. Now git before I call the law."

Ironing the clothes and watching a soap opera on TV, Rita hears Gideon barking. She crosses over to the window and looks out. Seeing nothing, she returns to her ironing. Moments later, she hears Joe come in through the back door. He enters the living room from the kitchen with a moonshine jar in his hand. Rita watches him as he stumbles to his chair.

"Would you like something to eat, Joe?"

"Ain't hungry."

He takes a gulp of liquor as Rita continues to iron. She is cool, comforted by knowing the shotgun is just in the other room.

"What is this shit you're watching?"

"The Guiding Light."

"Well, turn it."

Rita stops her ironing and switches the channels. There are only two more and both are showing soap operas.

"What would you like me to turn it to?"

"Turn the Goddamn thing off."

He lights a cigarette.

"Where's the girl? Why ain't she in here helping you iron? She's old enough to work."

Rita hangs a shirt on the side of the ironing board and gets another one out of the basket.

"She's a young girl, Joe. She has friends. She needs to be with them some. Life shouldn't be so hard when you're young."

"She should be here helping you. Where'd she get money to go gallivanting? You give it to her?"

He gets up and goes into Lillian's room.

"Joe? What are you doing in there?"

"None of your Goddamn business."

Rita puts down the iron and follows him.

Lillian's room is like the rest of the house, clean, neat, and spare. A picture of Little Joe sits on one side of the vanity and a mason jar of pennies, resting atop the bankbook, sits on the other. Joe picks up the picture of Little Joe and stares at it wordlessly. He quickly puts it down when Rita walks in.

"You need to git on back in there and tend to your ironin'."

"Now, honey. What could you possibly want in here? Why there's nothing in here but girl stuff."

Joe ignores her and continues to look. He spies the penny jar, picks it up and discovering the bankbook, opens it.

"What the hell is this? Have you seen this? Do you know about this?"

Rita looks over Joe's shoulder.

"Why, no! What is it?"

Joe slams it in his hand.

"It's a bankbook! There's over three thousand Goddamned dollars in there! Where the hell did she git that? You raising a whore?"

Stunned, Rita says nothing. Her silence enrages Joe, and he thrusts his face into hers.

"You been giving her whoring lessons?"

Rita slaps him as hard as she can and Joe loses all reason. He punches her in the stomach and as she doubles up in pain, he hits her in the face. He shouts obscenities at her as he beats her. Grabbing her by the hair, he pulls her out of the room and into their own bedroom where he rapes her.

Rita lies on the bed, face down and partially dressed. Joe zips up his pants.

"Stupid bitch."

She moans. He crosses the room to the bureau and picks up a key out of a dish. He leaves, locking the door behind him. Rita rolls over onto her side and stares at the open window. The curtain gently billows over her. Stupid man, she thinks as she loses consciousness.

Joe drives the old truck down the driveway behind the house and into a copse, where the truck will be hidden from the house. He has a plan and it is not a nice one. He parks, gets out, and hikes back to the house.

Lillian parks the Indian and looks up at the office building. On the window upstairs are painted the words "Axel S. Drake, Attorney at Law. She walks in the building and up the stairs to the doorway with his name. She takes a deep breath, anxious about how to ask for help. The secretary greets her as she closes the door.

"I'm sorry, Lillian, but Mr. Drake is not here. He's in court today over at Wentworth."

"Will he be back today?"

"I believe so. Why don't you check back around 4:30?"

Lillian looks at the clock on the wall which reads 1:30.

"Is there anything I can do for you, sweetie? If you would like some money, he has some pre-signed checks for you."

Lillian shakes her head. She's not really sure what she wants except help for her mother.

"Would you like to leave a message in case he calls in?"

"No thanks, Can I use the telephone?"

"Sure, honey."

She turns the telephone toward Lillian so that she can reach it.

"I have to go to the little girl's room. Will you be all right out here by yourself?"

Lillian nods and the secretary leaves, giving her some privacy. She picks up the receiver and dials.

"Riley? Oh, Riley! I need to see you. Can you meet me at the river?"

"Sure, darling. Is everything all right?"

"No. It's all terrible, please come. Right now."

She hangs up the phone without waiting for a response and rushes down the stairs to the motorcycle.

Lillian pulls up to the fishing shack and sees Riley there waiting, sitting on the back of his car, drinking a Pepsi. He jumps off when he sees her and offers her the bottle. Lillian shakes her head and grabs onto Riley.

"Hey there. What's the matter?"

He moves a lock of hair out of her face.

"Daddy's gone crazy again. He kicked Mama down! Oh! Worse. I can't tell you. I'm so scared for her."

She starts to cry, the tears streaming down her face.

"Mama made me leave. She think's he'll hurt me."

Agitated, Riley runs his hand through his hair.

"Did you call the sheriff?"

Lillian looks at him through watery eyes.

"No. What am I supposed to tell him? Daddy kicked Mama down? He didn't have his gun, he didn't threaten to do anything. He was just so mean."

"Was he drinking?"

Lillian shrugs. She doesn't know much about alcohol or about drinking it.

"I guess. I don't know. I never knew he drank till that day we went to the beach."

Riley takes her by the arms.

"Well, he drinks and he drinks a lot."

"Mama told me he fights the curse of liquor every day. I guess he's been losing the battle lately."

"Well, I agree with your Mama. You need to stay away from him. Sometimes when men drink, they go crazy and you don't need to be around when he ain't in his right mind. Especially not if he's kicking your Mama around."

"Where can I go?"

"To Pearl's. Surely her Mama will take you in for a few days."

"They're gone for the week. Mama told me to go there, but I didn't tell her they weren't there."

"Well then go to a motel. You've got the money. Go to Pearl's when she gets back."

"Okay. I need to go back to the house to get my things."

She takes the key to the Indian from her back pocket and hands it to Riley.

"Can I borrow your car?"

"Sure. Call me when you get to the motel."

They swap keys and kisses, and Lillian turns to leave.

"Hey. He's not at home is he?"

"No. I don't think so. He left. I don't think he'll be back for a while."

"You want me to come with you?"

Lillian shakes her head.

"Just grab enough for tonight and get out. Your Mama can pack the rest and tell you when it's safe to come home. Okay?"

Lillian nods.

"Okay. It's okay. I'll call you as soon as it's okay."

Riley reluctantly lets her go.

Lillian stops in front of the house and looks around for her father's pickup. Seeing no sign of it, she steps onto the front porch and into the house. In the living room the TV is blaring. Rita's ironing is out, unfinished, the iron still plugged in. She notices the door to her parent's room is closed, and thinking her mother is taking a nap, she tiptoes to her own room. Immediately she notices that things on the vanity are misplaced. She walks to it and places her hand where the bankbook was.

"Looking for this?"

The deep sound of Joe's voice startles her. She swings around and sees him standing in the corner with the bank book in his hand.

"What are you doin' with that?"

He slinks closer and stands within arm's reach, trapping her.

"Where'd you get all that money? You been whoring around?"

Lillian backs up as her father gets closer and she can smell the liquor on his breath.

"Little Joe gave it to me."

He slaps her face.

"Don't you say his name, you little slut."

"But it's my money, Daddy."

"Shut up!"

He pushes her against the wall and she screams. Covering her mouth with his hand, he grinds his body into her's.

"You gonna give me that money?"

She struggles to push him away but he pins her to the wall even harder. She is truly afraid of what her daddy will do.

"Give me the money and I'll let you go."

Lillian nods and Joe relaxes his body just enough for her to shove him. She tries to get around him but he grabs her by the arm.

"You little bitch. You're just like your Mama."

She beats on him with her free hand. He slaps her and falls down with her on the bed.

She screams.

"Mama!"

Joe slaps her again and pulls at her clothes, trying to take them off her.

"She ain't coming. I done fixed her."

They continue to struggle until a loud gunshot goes off and bits of shredded wood fall from the bead board ceiling. Lillian and Joe look toward the doorway and see Rita standing, battered and bruised, with the shotgun in her hand.

"Get off my baby!"

"Mama!"

Joe is confused.

"How'd you get out?"

Rita steps closer.

"I said, GET OFF MY BABY!"

Joe gets off the bed as quick as he can and just stands there looking at Rita.

"Lillian! Get out of the house, NOW! Go get Sheriff McRae."

Lillian crawls off the bed, crying and runs from the room.

Joe regains his composure.

"You ain't gonna shoot me. Just put that gun down."

Rita jacks the round into the chamber. Joe takes a step closer and reaches for the gun.

"Stop!"

"We done been through this. Give me the gun before I take it from you. You're gonna be sorry, you crazy ole bitch. Give it to me!"

Rita steadies the gun. Joe moves toward her, a smirk on his face.

"Yes, we've been here before and I told you what I would do, you sorry ass son of a bitch."

She pulls the trigger.

Rita is sitting in the swing with the shotgun in her lap when the sheriff arrives. He and the deputy get out of the car and walk onto the porch. Sheriff McRae looks at the deputy and nods his head toward the front door. He sits in the chair nearest the swing and the deputy goes into the house.

"Well, Rita. Is it over?"

She looks at him with blank eyes.

"I hope so, Bud."

Sheriff McRae pats her hand.

"It's gonna be all right, Rita."

Rita just sits there staring out into nothingness. For the first time in a long time, her mind is blank and she is not sure if she should be frightened or happy or sad. For a moment, the image of the beloved calico square in Mema's quilt comes to her. She quickly grabs onto it, finding comfort in the belief that something can come from nothing after all. That maybe she will make that quilt with Lillian. That she and Lillian can become something else entirely.

The ambulance comes and the paramedics gently lead her to it and help her into the back   Lillian and Riley arrive just as the ambulance leaves. Sheriff McRae meets them in the yard.

"Don't worry about your mother, sweetie. What she did was in self defense. I'll see to that."

Lillian, tired and emotionally drained, nods her head in understanding.

"I imagine they're going to keep her in the hospital for a while, evaluate her and what not. I've got some ladies from the church coming over to clean up, bring you a little food. Do you want one of them to stay with you tonight?"

"No, I'll be okay. I just want a bath."

"If you change your mind, just let one of the ladies know"

He walks toward the squad car, then stops and turns toward Lillian.

"I almost forgot. Dr. Jenkins left you a bottle of pills, just in case you have trouble sleeping. They're on the kitchen table."

Lillian, overwhelmed by the kindness, breaks down in great big sobs. She runs to the sheriff, clings to him tightly and cries.

"Thank you. Thank you so much. Please don't let them hurt Mama."

The sheriff pats and rubs Lillian's back and speaks softly to her, the way you would calm a wild animal.

"I'll take care of her, I promise you will see her smiling that sweet smile at you in no time at all. As soon as I get back to the office, I'll call Sean McDowell. He'll want to know. He'll want to help."

He peels Lillian's arms off of him and takes her hand in his.

"Now, you go back in there, take those pills, get you a bath, and go to bed. There ain't nothing more you can do to help your Mama than let her know you're gonna be okay. She needs to be thinking of herself right now and not worrying about you. Understand?"

"Yes."

He kisses the top of her head.

"It's gonna be all right. Now let me go. I got work to do."

Lillian, still scared, shaken, and stunned, is reluctant to let him go. She suddenly realizes everything she has lost; her beloved brother, her daddy, her innocence. She doesn't want to be alone with all that loss. She can't be, she thinks. Just as the tears begin to flow again, she feels a warm, familiar arm on her shoulder, gently pulling her toward him. Riley is still here. He is here for her. She leans into him.

"Stay here with me tonight."

"I wasn't planning on leaving, darlin'."

SOPHIA

Grandma Rita proved herself to be a true red dirt girl. Lots of grit as Sheriff McRae would say. Mr. McDowell came to see her everyday in the hospital and they got married not long after Grandpa's funeral and moved to Virginia. No one blamed her for what had happened or for finding happiness out of it, but her family missed her, especially Mama, who grieving with all that loss, discovered that she wasn't so alone after all. Daddy had given her me and she threw herself into motherhood as much as she had thrown herself into being an actress.

Book 3

############### CHAPTER 10 ###############

And I am Born

1967

The morning air is heavy with wet red dust, churned up by all the plowing that the farmers do at the same time every morning, every day, every year in the spring. The fine particles dance high in the sky for a while, then begin to settle, soaking up the heavy moisture that lays close to the ground, making it hard to breathe and hard to move. Some people call it being lazy. Some people go on about their business, moving steady but slow. Lillian knows that all that hot, heavy, wet air just wants to hold you down, keeping you in your place, sucking the ambition and energy from you.

But then, she's very pregnant, large and round and heavy, so everything weighs her down. She's spread out, no, sprawled is a better word, on the porch swing of the old house, her tent-like, sack-like faded floral dress hiked up to mid-thigh in an effort to lighten the burden of her heaviness. Hair in a pony tail, chewed fingernails, still a girl, but now with a woman's body. She doesn't have the energy to push the swing so she just lays there slowly rubbing her belly with one hand and smoking a cigarette with the other.

Pearl, ever stylish in a hot pink, boldly flowered mini dress, sits in the worn ladder back porch chair, Little Joe's guitar held like the precious object it is in her hands. Absentmindedly, she strums the strings, no particular tune, just random chords that come into her head as she sits there, quiet, waiting for Lillian to speak and finally she does.

"Well, tell me all about college, Pearl. Is it hard? Do you get homesick any?"

Pearl smiles at her cousin.

"I wouldn't call it hard, exactly. There's so much to learn and know about. I never knew the world was such a big place. It's different everywhere you go."

Lillian frowns, the thought of being out in the world, of seeing the world, of losing that dream almost overwhelms her.

"I wouldn't know about that seeing as how I reckon I'm stuck here for the rest of my life."

Pearl stops strumming, aware of the horrible mistake she has made.

"Oh, Lillian. Don't say that! You have your whole life ahead of you…a good husband who loves you, a new baby coming. That's what life is all about. Just what you have. Not where you go or where you live."

"You sound like Mama."

Pearl puts down the guitar, straightens her tiny dress, and changes the subject.

"Are they going to let you finish school this year?"

Lillian winces, a sudden sharp pain in her belly. She sits half way up.

"I don't know. I'm still waiting for a decision."

There's another sharp pain, longer now, and more intense. She stands up.

"I'm not feeling real good, Pearl. Walk with me, will you?"

Pearl jumps up and grabs Lillian's arm.

"Is the baby coming? Is it time, yet?"

Another contraction hits Lillian. She tenses and moans, sure now that soon the baby will be in her arms. Pearl doesn't wait to be told. She runs into the house, slamming the old screen door behind her.

"I'm calling Riley."

"Okay. Tell him to hurry."

The inside of the county hospital is green. Green walls, green lights, even greenish floor tiles. The waiting room is stark with a few uncomfortable chairs and a table with a few magazines on it and an overflowing ashtray. Riley, his one good suit crumpled, chain-smokes, creating a cloud near the ceiling of the spare room. He's worried about Lillian, about the baby, about being a father. So strange he thinks, that just yesterday, he was a boy trying to impress a girl, now he's a man, with a man's troubles when all he really wants is to be that boy again. Now Lillian. Now a baby.

He stubs out the cigarette and lights another one.

"I didn't think it would take this long. What's it been? Six hours? Seven?"

Pearl sits calmly and quietly reading a magazine.

"It takes a long time in the movies."

Riley laughs.

"Yeah, I reckon it does."

"Do you want a boy or a girl?"

Riley blows out a trail of smoke and answers quickly, no doubt in his mind.

"Boy."

He stands up and walks to a door with a little wired window at the top. He looks through it and sees nothing but an empty green hallway. He paces, smoking short, hurried puffs from his cigarette.

"Hope she's okay."

Pearl nods.

"I'm sure she is."

Inside the labor room, Lillian, hair soaked, lies in hard labor on the narrow hospital bed. A long, intense contraction doubles her body and a kind nurse pats her face with a cool wet rag.

"I swear I'll kill him if he ever touches me again."

The nurse chuckles and pats her arm affectionately.

"You'll change your mind, honey. Once that little baby comes out, that's all you'll think about. You won't remember any of this. Before you know it you'll be back in here with another one."

Lillian wants to slap that nurse, but she doesn't. She just pushes, extra hard now, anxious to rid herself of Riley's passion.

Two hours later, a smiling, happy Lillian sits up in her hospital bed, a bedside tray of partially eaten food in front of her. Riley, his worries gone now, holds the baby so that Pearl can see her. He is smitten.

"She's the most beautiful thing I've ever seen!"

Pearl rubs the side of her tiny, red face.

"Oh, she is! What are you going to call her?"

She looks to Riley, then to Lillian.

"I'm going to call her Sophia. Sophia Loren Reynolds."

A few weeks later, Lillian, wearing an old maternity dress, paces the floor of the untidy living room with a screaming Sophia The ironing board stands in a corner with clothes scattered about it, movie star magazines litter the sofa and the end tables. The ashtray overflows, cigarette butts spilling out onto the coffee table. Lillian pats and pats the baby but she only screams louder.

"Come on, Sophia, hush now. Shhhhhhh. There ain't nothing to cry about. You just ate so you can't be hungry. No, you can't."

She looks at the clock over the sofa which reads 1:30.

"You don't eat again til 4:30."

She jiggles and pats the colicky baby but there is no soothing her. The telephone rings and Lillian juggles the baby and the phone.

"Hello? Hold on. I can't hear you."

She puts Sophia in the cradle and returns to the phone.

"Okay, I'm back."

She puts a finger in her ear to mute the sound of the crying baby.

"Lillian? This is Mrs. Dalton from Senior High. I'm calling to confirm that you WILL be enrolling for the next term?"

Sophia wails louder and Lillian becomes agitated. She keeps looking at the baby, saying nothing. What can she say? What should she say? How can she possibly go to school? She looks around the room and sees the clutter, her utter failure at motherhood and housekeeping.

"Lillian? Are you still there?"

"Yes, Mrs. Dalton. I'm here. I don't think I can just yet. Maybe the term after that?"

Making that decision does not bring the relief she hoped it would. Now she's a school failure as well. Adult life is hard, especially for a girl and especially hard for a girl with a crying infant.

"All right, Lillian. I'll give you a call back next term."

"Thank you, Mrs. Dalton."

She hangs up the phone and looks at the crying baby. She grabs her cigarette pack and lighter and runs to the door and onto the porch where she lights a cigarette. She puts her hands over her ears but she can't escape the sound of the baby.

"Please, God. Make her shut up just for a minute."

She's never asked God for much and she halfway believes a cone of silence will fall over her, but that doesn't happen so she goes back inside and turns on the television.

Two hours later, the TV is blaring, trying to drown out the sound and Lillian tries desperately to get Sophia to drink her bottle. But the baby hollers and spits out the nipple. She walks and shakes and rocks and cajoles, but Sophia still cries. Frustrated now, exhausted, sleep deprived and desperate, Lillian picks up the baby and shakes her.

"What's the matter with you?"

The baby screams and Lillian lays her in the cradle and runs into her bedroom. She rummages through a bureau drawer, the sounds of the TV and the baby crying just as loud in here. She finds the bottle of pills the doctor gave her the night her mama shot her daddy. She shakes out one, hesitates for a moment, then shakes out another. She pops them in her mouth and swallows them, not sure what they will do, but having faith that they will somehow help her get through the afternoon. Fortified, she calmly walks into the living room, lies down on the sofa and closes her eyes.

After an extra long day at work, Riley comes home to find Sophia screaming, the TV blaring, the house in disarray and Lillian passed out on the sofa. He rushes to the baby and picks her up, then tries to wake Lillian.

"Lillian. Lillian, honey. Wake up."

She stirs, then seeing Riley with the baby sits up and rubs her eyes.

"She won't stop cryin'. She's been cryin' all day."

Riley has the baby on his shoulder. He bounces up and down and pats her as she whimpers.

"Why didn't you call the doctor? She's burning up."

Lillian is angry now. Angry at Riley, at Sophia and at herself. Angry at missing the obvious.

"And how was I supposed to get there? On the Indian?"

"Honey, you could have called me."

Lillian doesn't respond. Just hangs her head.

Riley kisses the top of her head.

"It's all right. I'll get you a car tomorrow. I don't know what I was thinking. You being out here all alone. Take the baby. I'll call the doctor."

It was just colic after all. A rough baby for a first time mother. The next day Riley bought Lillian a very well used but functional station wagon for the new family and Lillian pushed the Indian motorcycle into a shed and covered it carefully with a sheet of canvas. She closed the doors and locked them, leaned her forehead against the door and sighed deeply. There would be no more riding the wind for her. Girlhood was over, without a doubt. It was time to grow up.

############### CHAPTER 11 ###############

A Growing Family

1970

Over the past few years, Lillian has become a better housekeeper. The kitchen is shining brightly but clutter is still a problem. Clean dishes lie next to the sink and on the stove, a broom and mop stand propped against a cabinet, kid's toys are scattered around the floor. But she has three children now. The twin girls, Gina and Lola are just six months old and Sophia is two and a half. Life is busier now than she could ever imagine and it is rare that she has a moment to herself.

Pearl, sporting a new hairdo and stylish dress, sits at the kitchen table holding Sophia on her lap. The twins happily sit in high chairs while Lillian, drinking a beer, shoves tiny spoonfuls of baby food into their birdlike mouths. They have food on their faces, their bibs and their high chairs but no one cares.

"I have some real good news, Lillian."

Lillian tries to get Gina to eat a spoonful of carrots.

"Open up, Gina, honey."

She looks at Pearl with a grin.

"You and Kevin gettin' married?"

Pearl laughs and bounces Sophia and tickles her.

"We're not in any hurry for that!"

"Well, you're going to have to get around to it one of these days if you want any of these little darlins."

She feeds Lola a bite.

"Ain't that right, Little Lola."

Looking at Pearl, "What is it, this good news?"

"I got a record contract!"

"No!! You're kidding!!"

She puts the spoon in the baby food jar and walks over to Pearl, giving her and Sophia a great big hug.

"I can't believe it! Course, I always knew you would do it."

She hugs Pearl again.

"I'm so proud of you! Oh, I know Little Joe is in heaven looking down and he's proud, too!"

"I keep his letter in the guitar case."

The girls fall silent for a moment in memory of Little Joe.

"Did you ever read yours?"

Lillian resumes feeding the children and chugs the rest of her beer.

"No. Not going to, either."

"Oh, Lillian. I'm so sorry I brought it up."

Lillian continues to shove food into Gina and Lola, her thoughts consumed by her brother and the life she once wanted, but she pulls herself out of it.

"So, what's this record deal about?"

"It's the one song, really. The one Kevin wrote for me. Like a test, I suppose, but it's real. We recorded the record two weeks ago."

"Well, shoo wee. I guess I'll be singing along with you on the radio."

Lillian shoves a last bite into the mouth of Lola and immediately scrubs the tiny face with a damp diaper. She repeats the process with Gina.

"I reckon you'll be famous and long gone from here soon enough. We'll just be an old memory."

Pearl takes the diaper from her, hugs her neck and whispers.

"I'll never forget you, Lillian and I'll never be far away. I promise. You're my best friend."

Lillian takes two bottles of beer from the refrigerator, opens them and hands one to Pearl.

"To best friends."

"Yes. To best friends."

That night, the girls in bed, finally asleep, Lillian puts away the clean dishes when the phone rings.

"Hello?"

It's Riley. He's sitting in his office at the car dealership looking at a pretty woman trying to buy a car. He locks eyes with her and flashes his best charming smile.

"Hey, Honey. Don't wait up for me. It's going to be a late night. Just wanted to let you know."

"Riley..."

"Gotta go. Got a customer"

He hangs up the phone.

Lillian doesn't know about the pretty woman customer. Can't even imagine such a thing. Riley works so hard for their family. All she can think about is how tired he will be when he comes home. She walks slowly and quietly to the girl's small bedroom - her old bedroom, only now it is crowded with baby stuff and kid stuff and furniture. She wonders if she had so many toys when she was a girl. She doesn't remember.

The babies lie in their cribs and Sophia is curled up in her big girl bed. Lillian kisses each one, then draws the curtains closed and walks quietly out of the room. She whispers.

"Sweet dreams, babies."

She walks to the fireplace mantle and picks up Little Joe's sealed letter, goes into the kitchen for a six pack of beer, then heads for the porch swing where she lights up one of Riley's joints. She sits there, swinging slightly, chugging beer, smoking, and staring at the unopened letter. She is unbelievably sad and fighting it as hard as she can. Why, oh, why did Little Joe have to die and how, oh, how did she end up here with a house full of kids? Why does she feel so lonely? Why does she feel like life is passing her by and she is just watching it go, unable to stop it or slow it down?

A familiar voice comes out on the radio. It's Pearl and her new song. Beautiful Pearl, whose every dream comes true, who she really, really loves. Best friend Pearl, but she can't bear to hear that song on the radio so she turns it off and mumbles.

"I'm so sorry, Pearl."

1973

The early morning light penetrates through the sheer curtains in Lillian and Riley's bedroom. Lillian lies in the bed alone, a full ashtray, movie magazines and pill bottles litter the bedside table. She can hear the sound of the children crying and fighting and the loud TV and she covers her head and snuggles back into the blankets. Riley knocks on the door and she moans.

"Lillian. We're going to be late."

She wakes up and peers at the clock, which reads 6:30. She groans, then sits up on the side of the bed. She runs her hands over her face and hair and slowly rises from the bed. She puts on a robe and stumbles out the door and into the kitchen.

Sophia, Gina, Lola, and the new child, Brigitte, are eating breakfast at the table. Sophia, six now and dressed in mismatched clothes sings her ABC's while stirring her cereal with her spoon. Gina and Lola, just four, are still in their pajamas and are fighting over vitamins. Riley, bless his heart, is frying eggs, oblivious to the noise.

Gina cries and grabs at Lola's closed hand.

"I want Pebbles. It's my turn!"

Lola holds her closed hand further away.

"No!"

Gina cries louder.

"Give it to me!"

Watching the fight, two-year-old Brigitte begins to cry, too.

"Mama. Mama. I want Mama."

Lillian picks up Brigitte and addresses the twins.

"What's going with you two?"

"She won't give me Pebbles. I want Pebbles."

Lillian picks up the vitamin jar and shakes out the characters until she finds a Pebbles.

"Here you go, Sweetie. Now give me back Fred."

Gina gives Fred to Lillian and chews her Pebbles. Lillian sits at the table, still holding Brigitte and looks at Riley.

"So, when did you come home? This morning? You look like you're in the same clothes."

He finishes his egg and puts it on a plate, adds salt and pepper and throws on bacon. He flashes his car salesman smile at Lillian.

"I reckon I got in about two, maybe three. It's hard to leave a good game of poker. Especially when you're winning."

Well. You didn't come to bed. Again."

Riley picks up a second fully laden plate and puts it in front of Lillian. He sits in the empty chair and begins to eat.

"I slept on the couch."

Sophia pipes up.

"And I waked him up!"

"Woke him up, honey. You woke him up."

Sophia nods her head emphatically.

"And you know why? So he can go to school with me. Right, Mama?"

Lillian rubs the top of Sophia's head.

"That's right, sugar. Okay, girls. I want everybody to go and get dressed. Gina, Lola. Your clothes are on the bed."

Sophia squirms.

"But I am dressed, Mama."

I know you are honey, but Grandma Dunn sent you a pretty new dress to wear for your first day at school. Don't you remember?"

Sophia nods and with a sad face, turns the nod into a shake.

"But I don't like to wear dresses."

"Well, I tell you what. You wear that pretty little dress today, so we can take your picture and all, then you can wear whatever you want tomorrow. Is that a deal?"

Sophia nods and leaves the table. Lillian lowers her voice and addresses Riley.

"Dr. Jenkins called me yesterday."

"And..."

"I'm pregnant again. I ain't having any more kids after this. Even if it's a girl. No more."

*************** Chapter 12 ***************

Wild Indians

1977

It's a hot, hazy summer day and Lillian and the girls are shucking a large pile of sweet corn in the shade of the old crape myrtle tree. The youngest girl, Raquel, just four, and her sister Brigitte play near the garden. Raquel picks up a funny shaped rock and shows it to Brigitte.

"Show Mama."

Raquel clutches it in her hand and runs to Lillian.

"Mama! Look what I found!"

Lillian pauses her shucking, wipes her face with the back of her hand and smiles.

"What is it, Raquel? A worm?"

"Ewww Mama. No!"

Raquel shakes her head and thrusts out her hand, red from the garden dirt. Brigitte picks it out of her palm.

"It's an arrowhead! Grandma Dunn said wild Indians used to live all round here."

Lillian takes the arrowhead from Raquel and turns it over.

"Well, I haven't seen one of these in a while. We used to find them all the time."

"Did you know any wild Indians, Mama?"

Ten-year-old Sophia laughs.

"Grandma said Mama was a wild Indian."

"Is it yours, Mama?"

The older girls laugh, but Lillian is upset.

"No! And I was not a wild Indian. What else did Grandma say?"

Sophia reaches for another ear of corn.

"She said when you weren't running wild, you were pretending. She said you were always pretending."

Brigitte leans on her mother.

"What did you pretend, Mama?"

"Well, I reckon, just about anything. But mostly, I pretended to be a famous movie star."

She makes the movie star pose she used to make when she was a girl and her children laugh at her, Raquel laughing the loudest.

"You're silly, Mama!"

Agitated, Lillian starts shucking another ear of corn.

"Yes, I am. And I was a silly girl, too, always wantin' somethin' I could never have."

Sophia recognizes the agitation in her mother but wants to know more.

"What do you want now, Mama?"

Lillian stands up and brushes off the stray corn silk.

"I want y'all to finish shucking this corn while I start supper."

The girls collectively moan as Lillian hurries away.

That evening, Lillian prepares the corn for canning. In the kitchen, the old pressure canner hisses loudly on the stove. The sound of the playing girls fights to be heard over the loud TV.

Lillian, cutting corn off the cob, knocks over her beer as she reaches for her cigarette. She just stands there, watching it flow down the slope of the kitchen floor and under the stove. She checks the time on the clock before going to the door to call her daughter.

"Sophia! Come here, please."

She grabs another beer from the fridge and opens it, leaving the small stream to dry by itself on the floor. She resumes cutting the corn and Sophia pops her head in the door.

"Yes, Mama?"

"What are y'all doing in there?"

Sophia walks into the kitchen, stepping over the rivulet of beer.

"It's a surprise for you."

"What kind of surprise? Y'all ain't tearing up the house, are you?"

Sophia smiles, big and happy.

"No, Ma'am. You'll see."

Lillian slices the corn off the last cob.

"Do you think you can help me clean up in here before Daddy gets home?"

Sophia nods her head and starts throwing the empty corn cobs away.

"Don't go in the living room. You'll mess up the surprise."

Lillian takes a long swallow of her beer and watches the back of her daughter as she diligently cleans the table, wondering what in the world she is up to. How was she so lucky to have such a sweet girl for a daughter… always thoughtful and helpful. How would she get by without her. Sometimes Lillian felt like Sophia was the sober adult and she, Lillian, was still a wild Indian. Maybe time got things wrong sometimes.

In the living room, the furniture has been moved and a rope stretched across the room has an old quilt clothes-pinned to it. The girls are in various stages of pretend with funky makeup, and teased hair. Gina is dressed in Lillian's clothes with a very stuffed bra and Raquel has a mustache drawn on her upper lip.

Gina hears a car and looks out the window.

"It's Daddy!"

The girls continue to fix each other up as Riley comes through the door.

"Hey. What's going on here?"

Raquel runs to Riley who picks her up and rubs her mustache.

"What's this?"

"It's a mutach. I'm a man. What's this?"

She touches a pink spot on Riley's shirt. He tickles her and puts her down.

"Where's Mama? In the kitchen?"

Lola nods.

"She's fixing supper."

Brigitte pokes her head out from around the quilt curtain with her finger to her mouth.

"Don't tell Mama! It's a surprise."

Riley smiles, loosens his tie and heads into the bedroom.

"I hope she likes it!"

Finally, all the preparation is over and the girls are ready to put on their surprise for Lillian. Sophia sits Riley in his chair and the other girls stand behind the quilt. Sophia calls to her mother.

"Okay, Mama. You can come in now. Close your eyes."

Lillian stumbles in with her hand over her eyes. When she is through the doorway, she removes her hand and, eyes wide, mouth open, gasps. She recovers her shock and sits on the arm of Riley's chair as the show begins, repeatedly pulling her thumb in and out of her beer bottle.

Sophia comes from behind the curtain and bows. She is dressed in an old suit of Riley's, her hair tied up and under a hat.

"Ladies and Gentlemen, Mama and Daddy. Welcome to our fashion show."

She bows again before continuing.

"The most famous movie stars in the world have agreed to entertain you right here in your living room."

A final bow and she swings her arm out to introduce the first movie star. Riley cheers and claps but Lillian remembers when she and Pearl were preparing a similar show. How mad her Daddy was. How he pointed his finger at her and yelled.

"I ain't telling you again. Quit your silly pretending..."

The girls line up to sing. They hold hands and bow at the end of the song and Riley claps and cheers again but Lillian is quiet.

"Well now. That was mighty fine, girls, mighty fine."

Lillian has seen nothing her daughters are doing but feels the shame, over and over again, her face becoming flushed with the memory.

"What'd you say, Mama? Think we have some future movie stars?"

It's too much for Lillian. She jumps off the arm of the chair, yelling as she goes.

"Y'all need to quit this silly pretending."

Riley grabs her arm.

"Honey. They thought you'd be happy."

She shakes his hand off her arm.

"Well, I'm not. Just leave me alone. Please."

She runs into the kitchen and grabs a beer.

Oh, God. What is the matter with me? Why does everything have to be so hard. They are just girls, just playing. I hate you, Daddy. I hate you.

She sits at the table, lays her head in her arms and cries.

*************** Chapter 13 ***************

Lipstick on his Collar

Lillian stands at the kitchen door watching the storm clouds swell. It'll rain soon and there's the laundry to do. The never ending laundry. Gideon is sprawled out in front of the old shed, grateful that the sun has gone behind the clouds and the air is cooler. He's an old dog now and spends most of his time napping. Lillian grabs a key from the hook by the door and runs to the shed. She unlocks the padlock and opens the door. The Indian is still there, still covered by the large canvas sheet. She stares at it for a moment, then pulls back the cover, rubbing her hands along the shiny metal. She stands back and studies it, remembering her ride with Little Joe, remembering what it felt like to be free, with the wind in your hair. She climbs on the seat and pretends to drive.

Sophia has followed her mother and stands in the doorway watching her.

"You going for a ride, Mama?"

Lillian hesitates before getting off, reluctant to give up her dream.

"No. I was just remembering what it was like to be a girl. Sometimes I forget."

She reaches for the canvas and Sophia rushes to help her.

"I want a memory, too, Mama. One day, will you take me for a ride?"

Lillian shuts the door, locks the padlock and pockets the key. She rubs the top of Sophia's head.

"Maybe."

"Before I get old?"

"Maybe. I said, maybe. Get back to the house before it starts to rain."

"You coming, Mama?"

"In a bit. Go on, now."

She wants some time to herself, not much, but just enough to reclaim that lost energy she can't ever seem to find. She feels old and she's only twenty-seven. She sits under the crape myrtle tree and calls to old Gideon who lumbers over to her and plops down with his head in her lap, like the old days when they were both young. Such a good old dog. not many more years left in him, she thinks. Another piece of her girlhood soon to go. This is what life is, she reckons, at least for her.

Piece by piece, you lose yourself until you are someone else entirely. She wonders who that will be. Not some old crotchety woman, she hopes, but maybe someone like her mother. She misses her mother, but she's glad she is happy with Mr. McDowell. Maybe she and the kids can go visit one day. She'd like to see Mama again. Lay her head in her lap or watch her brush her long, long grey hair. See her twinkling green eyes. Steal some of that strength she has. The rain has finally started to come down and she gets up, ready to tackle the day.

Three large laundry baskets, overflowing with dirty clothes sit on the kitchen floor. Raquel helps Lillian sort the clothes into color piles. Gina, Lola, and Brigitte color at the table while Sophia makes a peanut butter and jelly sandwich on the counter top. The never-ending TV chatter from the living room invades the space. Lillian holds up a white shirt.

"See, honey. I want you to put all the white ones in a pile right here. I'll do the colored ones."

Raquel picks up a shirt and puts it on the floor.

"Like this, Mama?"

"That's real good, sugar."

Sophia sits at the table with her sandwich.

"Why can't we have a washing machine? My friend, Mary, has one right in the kitchen."

Well, I'm not saying it wouldn't be nice. Lord knows anything's better than going to the laundry mat with five young'uns and a pile of dirty clothes."

Raquel pulls out the shirt with the pink stain on it. Lillian notices it and takes it from her. She rubs it with her finger and watches it smear. A frown crosses her face.

Sophia swings her thin legs.

"Why don't we get one, then?"

"We can't afford it, hon."

She puts the shirt to her face and sniffs. Lillian puts her hand to her mouth and chokes back an alarmed cry. She stands up, rushes to her bedroom and flings open one of Riley's drawers. In it, near the bottom, she finds a "Playboy" magazine, the cover depicting the joys of "swinging". She flips through it, disgusted that Riley could read such filth. She holds the magazine by the spine and shakes it to see if anything comes out and when nothing does, she carefully puts it back. She goes through each drawer but finds nothing else. Then she runs her hands under the mattress. Finding nothing again, she begins to search his closet, going through or patting down each of his pockets.

Finding nothing still, but undaunted, she goes through the floor of his closet, opening his shoeboxes, removing the shoes and the paper. In one, she finds no shoes, but hundreds of receipts. She picks up one receipt from a motel, then another which reads "Elsie's Lingerie".

"I'll be damned."

She replaces the lid and moves to the bed where she starts organizing the receipts. She picks one up. It reads "Sharpe Jewelers". Another one, "Dina's Dress Shop". Trembling and sobbing, she places her hand on her heart for she knows these are not things for her and her heart is pounding. She breaks out in a sweat and wonders if she is having a heart attack.

"Oh, please."

Gasping for breath, she gets off the bed, grabs her pill bottle and pours two into her hand. Sophia stands in the doorway, looking at her Mama, then at the receipts on the bed.

"You okay, Mama?"

Lillian tries to compose herself and smile.

"I'm okay, sweetie."

Sophia glances around the room and sees the open drawers and shoeboxes with the contents on the floor.

"Mama?"

Wiping her face and collecting herself, Lillian walks over to Sophia and bends down. She adjusts the collar on Sophia's shirt and messes with her hair.

"I'm fine. I was just readin' some things that made me real sad. Kind of like how you cried when Charlotte, the spider died. You remember?"

Sophia nods, not quite convinced, and continues to look at her mother.

"Go on back in the kitchen. I'll be there in just a minute. Let me get these things together."

What do I do? How can this be happening? She gathers the receipts and puts them back in the box. All this time. I am such a fool. So stupid. So stupid. So stupid.

She pours out two more pills from the bottle and back in the kitchen, swallows them down with a beer. She stares at the clothes which have been sorted into two piles, white and colored, and focuses on the pink stain on the shirt. It's lipstick and it's not mine, she thinks. He's having an affair, he must be. He's horrible. How could he do this to us?

She finishes the beer and gets another one from the fridge. She glances at the time. It's 1:30. Gina, Lola and Brigitte are playing "go fish" at one end of the table. Lillian takes the shoebox and starts sorting the receipts into piles. She records the amount of each receipt into Sophia's spiral bound school notebook.

She continues to drink but neither the drink nor the pills can numb her shock. She finds a deposit slip receipt and studies it for a moment, then sets it aside. She is sure it is not from their account. She walks over to the telephone and looks up the number for Hometown Bank and Trust Co. from the yellow phone book. Finding it, she dials the number.

"Hometown Bank and Trust. Can I help you?"

"Yes, please. This is Lillian Reynolds. I need to write a counter check and I want to make sure that I have the correct account number."

"All right, Mrs. Reynolds, if you read that number out to me, I'll try to help you."

"It's 545378655 and my husband's name is Riley E. Reynolds.

It seems like an eternity before the woman answers.

"Mrs. Reynolds, I'm sorry but it seems that you are not authorized to sign checks on that account. I have another account here though, that has your signature. Would you like that number?"

Lillian closes her eyes and shakes her head.

"Yes, please."

"All right. That's 54387211. Is there anything else I can help you with today?"

"No, that's all I needed. Thank you."

Hanging up the phone, she looks at the clock. It's 3:30. She returns to the table and resumes her adding. Gina, Lola, and Brigitte pause in their game and stare at her but, Lillian, lost in her hurt, ignores them.

The TV is loud, louder than the children, who sensing something is wrong, play quietly. The empty shoebox hovers on the edge of the table and all of the receipts are in piles. Lillian reviews the figures in the notebook. Riley has spent $12, 354.85 on motels, $2,145.34 on restaurants, $1,788.82 on clothing, $962.58 on jewelry, and $826.94 on miscellanies. That's a grand total of $18,078.53. She circles that number several times, harder with each loop until the pencil point breaks. The phone rings, startling her, and she gets up to answer it, taking her beer with her.

"Hello?"

"Hey, Hon. You started supper yet?"

It's Riley. Lillian is so angry that she is numb, she can't talk and doesn't want to. She chugs her beer and checks the time. It's 4:05. How will she make it through the night?

"No."

"Good. Don't fix anything for me. We're having a big sales meeting tonight so I'll be late."

Lillian doesn't say anything, just chugs her beer. What do you say to your lying husband? Her mind is slow and dull, lulled into silence by the beer.

"Honey? Are you there?"

Another long swallow and the beer is gone. Lillian absently walks to the refrigerator.

"Yeah, I'm here."

"The meeting doesn't start until nine. I'll pro-"

Lillian interrupts him, tired of the sound of his voice and his lies.

"I gotta go."

She hangs up the phone, lights a cigarette and shuffles into the bedroom. What should I do, she thinks. What can I do? How can I do anything? How could this be happening? It can't be. But it is. On and on, her brain is alive now and she can't think. She grabs the Valium bottle and shakes out two, then another pill and pops them in her mouth. She sits on the edge of the bed waiting for the Valium to kick in, waiting for her brain to slow down just enough for her to think.

The clock reads 9:00 and Lillian feels better. She has a plan. She rushes into the kitchen, shuffles through the motel pile of receipts and selects the three most used. The kitchen is quiet, the girls have retreated to the living room and, dressed in their pajamas are watching TV.

"Okay girls. We're going for a ride. Everybody get up, go to the bathroom."

Sophia looks at her with somber eyes.

"Where're we going, Mama? Do we have to get dressed?"

Lillian puts bedroom shoes on sleepy Raquel then crosses the room and turns off the TV.

"We're going to get some ice cream."

The girls jump up, excited, and begin to speak at once.

"Y'all don't need to get dressed. Just put your bedroom shoes on."

Raquel rubs her eyes.

"Can I have chocolate?"

Gina and Lola chime in.

"I want vanilla with chocolate on top."

They giggle as Brigitte jumps up and down.

"Goody, goody, goody!"

Lillian hustles them all into the old station wagon, Sophia next to her and the rest piled into the back singing "There Was an Old Lady". Everyone is excited because ice cream is a rare treat. The kids just don't notice their mother is not smiling.

Lillian drives slowly to the dark lot of "Dan Brown's Ford" dealership. She turns in and circles the lot. There is no sign of activity. Sophia looks at her mother.

"This is where Daddy works. Why are we going here?"

"I thought he might like some ice cream, too. I don't think he's here, though. He'll just have to do without, I reckon."

She turns the car around and heads to the Dairy-O.

In the parking lot of the Dairy-O, the children enjoy their ice cream while Lillian looks at the motel receipts in her hand. The closest motel is the "Holiday Inn". Looking straight ahead, she sees it on the right. She starts the car and drives to the motel, circling, looking for Riley's car. Sophia licks her bubble gum flavored ice cream cone.

"Why are we going here?"

"I'm looking for something."

"What?"

Lillian is too sharp.

"None of your business. Eat your ice cream."

She circles a second time and doesn't see the car so she reads the second receipt which says "Colonial Motel."

Sophia knows something is going on with her mother. They have never gone out after dark for ice cream. And they never just ride around. And Mama is never this distracted.

"Where are we going now?"

Lillian glares at Sophia. How dare her question me, she thinks.

"We're just riding around. That's all you need to know right now."

She pulls out and heads down the road toward the Colonial Motel, where she again circles the parking lot. This time, at the far end, she sees Riley's car. Sophia sees it, too, and looks at her mother, concerned but saying nothing. Lillian puts the car in reverse and speeds out, seeking the comfort of home.

It's nearly dawn, the girls are asleep and Lillian sits in the dimly lit room smoking, a half empty gallon jug of wine on the floor beside her, an empty glass on the end table. Riley's packed suitcase sits beside the door. She did not take care to pack it carefully, she just threw the first things her hands touched in the bag including the Playboy magazine. She doesn't care, she hates him now.

She hears Riley's car followed by the sound of the keys in the door. He tiptoes into the house with his shoes in his hand. He is disheveled; hair messed up, tie hanging out of his pocket, shirttail out. He doesn't see Lillian sitting there in the dark waiting for him.

"I guess that was a pretty late meeting, huh?"

Riley is startled, but recovers. He stands his ground, prepared, always prepared for this moment.

"Honey? You didn't need to wait up. Is everything all right?"

Lillian puffs on her cigarette saying nothing.

"What's the matter, honey? Are the kids okay? Did you have a bad night?"

Lillian glares at him. Riley is confused. He walks over to the sofa and sits down. He unbuttons his shirt, avoiding Lillian's unblinking stare.

"Boy, I tell you. We had some meeting. It went on until two or three this morning. It was a doozy. I took a little nap in my office, honey, because-"

Lillian stands, fed up with his deception.

"Shut up!"

Riley looks up at her, amazed and confused because his charm is not working.

Lillian walks over and slaps him in the face, as hard as she can.

"Don't you ever call me honey again."

Riley bolts up and, grabbing her by the arm, shakes her.

"What in the hell has gotten into you?"

Lillian pulls away from him and picks up the suitcase. She opens the door and throws it outside as far as her anger will take it.

"I want you to get out of my house. I don't ever want to see you again."

She puts her hands over her face, crying.

"I can't believe I have been so stupid."

Riley touches Lillian's arm, trying to comfort her.

"Honey, whatever it is, we can work it out. Just tell me."

He puts both hands on her shoulders, hoping to bring her closer to him but she shrugs him off.

"DON'T TOUCH ME!"

Riley takes his hands off her and backs up.

"Okay, okay. I won't touch you. Just calm down. You're going to wake the kids."

Lillian remains standing by the open door, glaring at Riley. She straightens her shoulders.

"I know you did not have a sales meeting tonight. I know you were at the Colonial Motel. I know you are having an affair."

Riley runs his hands through his hair and expels a long breath. He puts his hands up, shakes his head and starts to speak but stops, out of words for once. He looks down at the floor.

Lillian continues.

"I want a divorce."

Riley is shocked and takes a step toward Lillian. She backs up and he stops.

"You can't mean that! We can't afford to get a divorce. What about the kids? And what will you do? You certainly can't work anywhere. You can't even clean up around here, you're so high on those pills all the time."

Lillian raises her arm to slap him again but he grabs it.

"You're just like your daddy."

"Get out of my house. Go back to your girlfriend. I don't want you here."

Riley shoves her arm back toward her and stomps out the door, slamming it behind him. Lillian sinks to the floor, crying and young Sophia stands in the doorway of her bedroom with tears in her watching eyes.

************** CHAPTER 14 ***************

A New Beginning

Sometimes, when life comes at you hard, there's nothing you can do but stand, or sit there and take it. Lillian, like her mother, fights back, as best as she can. With the kids at school, she sits in the porch swing, smoking, drinking a beer, and reflecting on her life. On where she would have been without Riley, gone far away maybe, but then, she would not have her girls, her precious girls, now fatherless, and she is determined to be the best mother she can be, even if it is with the help of cigarettes, alcohol and pills.

A cloud of dust follows the sound of a car driving slowly on the river rock driveway and it catches Lillian's attention. A brand new BMW convertible creeps along and Lillian, curious about who in the world this could be, slips out of the swing and walks over to the steps, hands shielding her eyes, straining to see the occupant of such a fancy car, now honking loudly, with a hand waving outside the driver's side window.

"Well, I'll be! Pearl!"

Lillians runs down the steps toward her cousin and best friend and throws her arms around her.

"I'm so happy to see you, honey!"

Pearl hugs her back.

"Me, too. Lillian. I came as soon as I could. It's hard being on the road."

"Well, I'm sure it is. Come on up here on the porch and tell me all about it. Can you stay long? Oh, I've missed you."

"Long enough, I reckon, for you to tell me all about it."

Pearl gives Lillian's arm a gentle squeeze as they climb the porch stairs and sit in their well accustomed places.

"Honey. I just can't imagine how much courage it took for you to kick Riley out. I mean, five kids, Lillian! I'm proud of you."

Lillian lights a cigarette and offers one to Pearl who declines.

"Well, I'm not brave. Stupid maybe, but I ain't livin' with someone who thinks sex ain't personal."

Pearl helps herself to a beer from the six pack on the porch and shakes her head in disbelief. The sunlight catches her diamond earrings throwing tiny rainbows over Lillian.

"I was mad about the money, too."

Lillian puts out her cigarette as Pearl laughs.

"I hate him."

"I reckon you do. I don't think much of him, either, now. Did he agree to the settlement terms?"

"Mr. Drake was very persuasive."

"Well, good! Now you can get a washer, like you always wanted."

Lillian lights another cigarette.

"I'm thinking about buying another house, moving into town, in one of those subdivisions. Mr. Drake said if I sell the farm, I could buy a right nice new house with two bathrooms, three or four bedrooms, even a dishwasher."

Pearl sets the straight back chair down with a thud.

"Oh, Lillian! Our great grandfather bought this farm."

"Well, he's dead and I'm gonna to be laying beside him if I don't get the hell out of here."

Pearls chugs the last of her beer, picks up her purse, pulls out tickets and hands them to Lillian.

"I'm going to be playing in Greensboro next month. I want you and the girls to be there. Y'all have never seen me play."

Lillians hesitates.

"Now, don't say no! I've reserved two rooms for us so you don't have to worry about driving home. Mama will be there, too, so she can help with the girls.

Lillian bursts into tears and covers her face with her hands.

"I haven't been five miles from this house since Riley took me to the beach. That was ten years ago! I wouldn't know how to act. Shoot, I wouldn't even know what to wear."

Pearl laughs sympathetically.

"You don't need to worry about that honey. I'm here for a few days. We'll go shopping. My treat. Hey."

She pokes Lillian's arm.

"Do you remember this?"

She sings.

> Hang down your head, Tom Dooley
> Hang down you head and cry

"Come on, sing it with me."

Lillian smiles at the memory of this long time favorite song and finally joins in.

> Hang down your head, Tom Dooley
> Poor boy, you're bound to die.

Lillian is excited for Pearl, but envious, too. Pearl's dream has come true and here she still is, more tied to the red dirt fields than ever. But she sings with Pearl, happy for her and glad to be something other than sad for even a little while.

That evening, after Pearl has left, Lillian pushes the furniture against the walls, clearing a small space in the middle of the living room. She puts Pearl's latest record on the turntable and turns the volume up as loud as it will go.

All five girls watch in awe as Lillian dances. They all sport new outfits and new hairdos and they drink Pepsi Cola, a rare treat, and the sugar and the music make their toes tap and their heads shake.

"Come on, girls. Let's have some fun! Dance with me."

And they do. They all whoop and holler and sing, stomping their feet, delirious with rare joy, until they collapse in a heap on the sofa, exhausted from such intense happiness.

I need to do this more often, thinks Lillian. Be happy. Make time to be happy. And she decides then, that she will sell the farm. She will buy that house in the tree-lined subdivision. She will have a washing machine and hell, why not, even a dryer. She pictures the house in her mind. Fresh and clean with large windows and a fenced in grassy yard for the girls to play in and for Gideon to grow old. Maybe a small garden, but maybe just big enough for a couple of tomato plants and lots of flowers. Zinnias, maybe. Her favorite. The butterflies like them and they are so colorful. But most of all, there is no red dirt, just green, green grass and a concrete driveway.

Yes. It feels good to be happy.

A few nights later, Lillian sits at the kitchen table, trying to study for the GED. She is distracted by thoughts of selling the farm and stares at the sealed envelope from Little Joe. Sophia, in her fluffy pink pajamas, stands in the doorway, watching her mother.

"Why don't you open the letter?"

Lillian studies her daughter for a moment. She is growing up so fast. Already she is almost as tall as Lillian and she is such a somber, thoughtful child. Not like her, not like Little Joe, not like Riley, and she realizes she doesn't know her at all. Her first little movie star daughter. She will be grown soon and how will I ever know her, she wonders.

"Because it will make me cry."

"Are you ever going to open it?"

"Maybe in the new house."

Sophia sees a rare opportunity to talk to her mother and she walks to the table, uninvited, and sits down.

"But, why do we have to move, Mama? I like our house."

"I know you do, honey, but I'm real tired of being a red dirt girl."

She puts her hand over her daughter's.

"I don't want you to dream of a better life. I want you to have one."

She gathers the books into a pile and places the letter on top.

"Besides, I'm tired of waitin' in line to go to the bathroom! Now, go to bed. I'll come tuck y'all in, in a minute."

Sophia wishes she had more time, but knows not to argue with Mama. She walks slowly out of the kitchen and when she gets to the doorway, she turns around and pauses.

"I love you, Mama."

Lillian is surprised and deeply touched.

"Why, I love you, too, Sophia."

Yes, Lillian thinks. It's time for us all to be happy.

The next day, the girls stand in a line watching Lillian back the Indian motorcycle out of the shed. She turns it around, facing the road and everybody jumps up and down, clapping, squealing like little girls do.

"Well, Sophia. You first. Come on and get on."

Sophia arranges herself in front of her mother, looks back at her and grins. Lillian's heart melts as she remembers her ride with Little Joe and she is excited to make Sophia as happy as she once was.

"Hold on tight! We're gonna ride the wind!"

And they take off, mother and daughter, finally sharing a real memory.

Later that night, when she thought the girls were asleep, Lillian walks down the driveway to the "for sale" sign, Gideon trailing behind her. Smiling, she places her hand on the sign and looks up toward the moon. She howls, long and loud, and Gideon joins in.

Sophia hears the howling, gets up from her bed and looks out the open window. Gina, sleeping, rouses.

"What is it?"

"Shhh. It's just Mama."

Gina sits up.

"Is she all right?"

"She's all right. She's singing with Gideon."

"Why's she doing that?"

"I reckon she's just happy. That's why. Go back to sleep."

CHAPTER 15

A Despicable Man

Chain smoking, Lillian sits on the edge of her chair on the other side of Axel Drake's desk. She is agitated and distraught for her world is coming apart.

"Let me get this straight. Riley is gone. No one knows where he is and he doesn't have to pay me. How can he do that? How can he just leave and no one knows where he is?"

Mr. Drake leans back in his chair.

"It happens all the time, Lillian. He is avoiding his responsibility by simply walking away. He still has to pay you, no matter where he is. But we can't make him if we can't find him and he knows that. I could find him with his social security number, but the law won't let me do that. So..."

He shrugs and holds up his hands.

"My hands are tied. I'm sorry. If you had the money, we could hire a private detective."

"I still have my money from Little Joe. Would that be enough?"

He leans forward, closer to the desk, closer to her.

"That may be all the money you have to live on, honey. Are you sure you want to do that?"

Lillian stubs out her cigarette and lights another one. Her hands tremble and she holds back the tears welling in her eyes.

"I don't know what to do."

Mr. Drake picks up a pen and writes a name on a piece of paper. He pushes it toward her.

"Go see this woman over at Social Services. Patricia Oliver. She might be able to arrange some help for you and the girls."

"Welfare, you mean."

"Now is not the time to let pride rule good sense. You go talk to her, see what kind of help she can offer."

He stands and walks over to Lillian who puts out her cigarette and prepares to leave.

"Meanwhile, I'll talk to Tim Smith. See how much he'll charge to do a little investigating."

Lillian takes his hand and shakes firmly.

"Thank you, Mr. Drake."

"You take care now. I'll give you a call in a few days and let you know what I've found out."

Lillian is distraught, but angry more than anything. Angry at Riley, who she loved and trusted and believed in. Angry, more, at herself, for daring to be content, daring to be happy as she was for a few days. Angry at life, at living, at everything. By the time she gets home the anger has turned into sadness. Plain, simple sadness.

The sun is low and Lillian is in the kitchen making peanut butter and jelly sandwiches for the girl's dinner when Raquel bursts into the room crying.

"MAMA!"

She runs to Lillian and grabs her leg. Lillian stoops to her level.

"What is it, honey? Are you hurt?"

She runs her hands quickly over Raquel's arms looking for hurts but Raquel is shaking her head.

"It's Gideon. I think he died cause he fell and he won't wake up."

She wails, louder now. Lillian hugs her and wipes at her tears.

"Shhh now. It's all right. Can you take me to him?"

Raquel stops crying and nods her head. Lillian takes her by the hand as Raquel leads her out the kitchen door.

The old hound dog lies on the ground, his head in Sophia's lap. Gina, Lola and Brigitte sit around him, petting him gently, all weeping softly. When Sophia sees Lillian she cries loudly.

"I think he's dead, Mama."

The girls make room for Lillian as she puts her hand on his chest, then his head. They wait expectantly as Lillian closes her eyes, holding back the tears. Raquel leans on Lillian's arm and cries to her.

"Is he dead, Mama?"

Lillian nods her head.

"Yes, I think he is."

She gently strokes him as all the girls sob and cry, truly sad at the passing of the old hound dog.

"He was a real good dog."

She and the girls mourn for a few minutes then she shoos them into the house, not wanting them to see the hole she has to dig or see her place his body into it.

But, Sophia watches from the kitchen window and she listens as a summer storm rumbles on the horizon. She watches her mother as she places stones on Gideon's grave. Lillian has made a wooden cross with the inscription "Gideon 1961-1977" and she hammers it into the head of the grave. Then she just sits there, looking at it as the wind picks up and the storm gets closer. Tears roll down her cheeks. The rain comes, but she stays, feeling like even God is crying with her, enveloping her with his tears.

Later that evening, when the storm is at its peak and lightening is flashing by the minute and the thunder is almost deafening, Sophia sits in her bed, knees to chest. Gina and Lola sit in theirs, covers to their chins and eyes wide with fear. Brigitte and Raquel hold hands in the doorway of the living room and cry.

Lillian sits stone-faced in front of a blaring TV. She yells at Brigitte and Raquel, Valium and alcohol giving a slur to her words and an edge of her Daddy.

"Goddamn it. I said go to bed. I'm tired of y'alls whinin'"

Brigitte talks back to Lillian.

"But, we're scared, Mama."

"Go to bed before I give you something to be scared of!"

Sophia yells from the bedroom.

"Come here. Y'all get in the bed with me."

Brigitte and Raquel run to Sophia's bed and she settles them in.

"Why don't we say our prayers?"

The small girls put their hands together under their chins and close their eyes. Sophia leads them in a prayer.

"Now I lay me down to sleep."

The others join in softly.

"And pray the Lord my soul to keep."

Lillian bangs on the wall.

"Y'all shut up in there. GO TO SLEEP!"

The girls continue to pray only softer.

"If I should die before I wake, I pray the Lord, my soul to take. Amen."

Sophia snuggles down into the covers.

"Now, let's all lay dawn and I'll tell a story."

The girls snuggle close to her.

"Once upon a time there was a beautiful princess..."

Brigitte interrupts.

"Was that Mama?"

"Shhh. Yes, it was Mama."

"Before she was mean?"

"I can't tell the story if y'all keep interrupting me."

Lillian stands just outside the doorway. The girls can't see her but she can hear them. She holds a cigarette and a glass of jug wine and cries softly.

"Anyway. It was Mama. Before she was mean, when she was a girl like us. She had long flowing hair, all the way to the floor and she was a thing to behold. One day she had a dream and in this dream..."

Lillian walks back to the living room, unable to listen to the rest of the story.

############### CHAPTER 16 ###############

The Concert

The day is bright and shines directly on Lillian's messy, cluttered and dirty kitchen. Pots, beer bottles, jug wine, an overflowing ashtray and the remains of the girls' breakfast litter the table, the countertops, the sink and the oven. The constant drone of the ever-present TV chatter floods the room. Lillian, wearing a faded floral housecoat, makes an attempt to clean up despite a hangover. She pops an aspirin and a Valium and chases them with orange juice. The phone rings and she looks at the clock. It reads 10:30.

"Hello."

It's Pearl, who is calling from a motel room.

"Hey, Lillian! It's me."

Lillian is happy to hear from her.

"Pearl! I thought you were on tour."

"I am. I was just thinking about you, honey. How are you doing?"

Lillian lights a cigarette.

"I guess I'm fine. Considering I feel like I'm trapped in one of your country music songs! No money, no love, no job, lots of kids. Hahaha! You ought to write one about me. You'd win an award."

She laughs sarcastically.

"Oh, Lillian. I guess you haven't found Riley?"

"No. Riley and his money are gone for good. And I say good riddance."

She puts out her cigarette and lights another one.

Pearl, sitting at the desk in the motel room twirls the cord in her hand. She looks up and toward the voice of a man just outside of the room.

"Come on, Pearl. We gotta roll."

"In a minute," mouths Pearl.

"Hey Lillian, I need to hang up. The bus is ready to go. You're still coming to the show, aren't you?"

"I wouldn't miss it. The girls are real excited, too. They can't wait to wear their new outfits."

"Well, come early. Go straight to the motel and tell them who you are. I put a room in your name and it's already paid for, so when you get there you can go on in. I don't know what time I'll get in town. By lunchtime, I hope."

The man appears in Pearl's doorway.

"Let's go."

"Okay! I'll see you tomorrow, honey. Bye."

"Bye, Pearl."

She hangs up the phone and sits at the table, her cigarette smoldering in the ashtray. Leaning her head in her hand, she picks nervously at her eyebrow and surveys her messy life. The sadness is overwhelming and she can't seem to find happiness anywhere. She lets out a mournful sigh.

The day drags on. The girls, home from school, have too much energy for Lillian. She takes the edge off by drinking jug wine and swallowing pills, anything to dull the sadness. She doesn't care that she is sad, she just doesn't want to feel like it is consuming her. But she does feel that way and nothing seems to dull the pain, no matter what she does.

By bedtime, her mind is fuzzy from the drink but still, she can't sleep. Her mind is agitated. She sits up in bed reading Good Housekeeping, a wine glass in her hand. The room is hazy with cigarette smoke and an open bottle of pills sits on the table beside the bed. She flips through the magazine, unable to concentrate and looks at the clock. It's 10:30.

She sighs, finishes her cigarette, then pops two pills. She hesitates a moment then pops a third. She turns out the light to sleep but with wide-open eyes she just stares into the darkness that will not numb her mind. She tosses and turns, first to her left then to her right, then onto her back staring blankly at the bead board ceiling. She can't escape herself. On and on her mind goes like the monkey chasing the weasel round and round the mulberry bush. A silly thought that won't go away. Finally, she throws off the covers, gets out of bed and rummages through the bottom of the closet till she finds her stack of old movie magazines, dating all the way back to when she was a girl. She takes them to the bed, pours herself another glass of wine and flips through the first one. The one with Marilyn Monroe on the cover.

The time ticks by slowly, but Lillian still cannot sleep. Her eyes are dark and heavy but when she closes them, it's like they're not closed at all but like something dancing just behind her eyelids, little explosions of colored lights, bursting into streams and bouncing off the back of her eyelids. Like her eyeballs are moving and won't be still. And her stubborn brain just won't let her rest. She drinks a glass of wine and takes a couple of pills and an hour somehow passes and still awake, she drinks more wine and pops more pills and reads more articles about the movie stars, which makes her sadder but she can't seem to get a grip and another hour passes and round and round she goes. Finally, in desperation, she takes four pills and chases them with a glass of wine and soon, the lights behind her eyes quit dancing, her brain slows and she falls asleep.

In the morning, the girls are excited about going to see Cousin Pearl. Sophia knocks on Lillian's door but there is no answer so she cracks open the door and peers in. She sees Lillian asleep on the bed, a movie magazine nearby. The bedside lamp is on, the wine jug is empty and the pill bottle is on its side. She shuts the door and tiptoes away.

The kitchen is strangely quiet without Lillian and the television chatter. The girls are dressed in their new outfits and sit at the table ready for breakfast to be over and their trip to begin. Sophia pours milk into their cereal bowls. Gina is ready to go and questions her big sister.

"Don't you think we should wake Mama up?'

Sophia looks at the clock, which reads 8:30.

"Let's wait until nine."

"But that's when we're supposed to leave."

"Shhh. I think Mama had a real bad night."

Gina is frustrated.

"Ohhhh!"

At nine, Sophia opens the bedroom door and walks quietly to the bed. She gently shakes Lillian, not really wanting to wake her. Afraid of her wrath but also scared to see her mother sleep so late. Lillian moans slightly.

"Mama. It's time to get up."

She shakes her again, a little rougher. Lillian moans again.

"Mama! Mama!"

Lillian is unresponsive so Sophia backs out of the door and heads back into the kitchen.

"She's still sleeping, y'all." We're going to have to wait. That's all."

The girls collectively groan, but Sophia gathers the dirty dishes and takes them to the sink.

"Y'all help me clean up so we'll be ready to go when she wakes up."

Sophia tries again at ten and at eleven, but Lillian won't wake up. She gathers the girls in the living room and turns on the television, sure the noise might wake Lillian and not worrying about whether or not she gets in trouble for waking her Mama.

At the motel where Pearl is staying, her mother, Helen, sits in the lobby reading "Southern Living". She glances up each time a guest comes through the door. Finally Pearl enters.

"Mom!"

Pearl puts down her suitcase and hugs her.

"I'm so excited you're here."

She looks around.

"Where's Lillian and the girls?"

"I don't know, Pearl. They haven't checked in yet."

Pearl looks at her watch.

"It's after noon! I hope they're okay."

"Maybe they slept in, knowing it's going to be a big night."

"Maybe."

In the hotel room, Helen unpacks Pearl's suitcase and garment bag. Pearl picks up the phone and calls Lillian's number. Sophia answers.

"Hello?"

"Hey, Sophia!"

Sophia breaks down and starts to cry.

"Oh, Pearl. Mama won't wake up."

Pearl sits down.

"Sophia?"

Sophia cries louder and the sobbing catches her breath, making it hard for her to talk.

"Sophia. Please, honey. I want you to listen to me. Can you do that?"

Sophia sobs and nods her head.

"Okay."

"Did you see your mother's pill bottle by the bed?"

"Yes."

"Were there any pills in the bottle? Did you look?"

"I think so. I don't know. It was laying down and the top was off."

Pearl closes her eyes and takes a slow breath.

"Okay, honey. I want you to go in there and try real hard to wake your mama up. Shake her really hard. Do you understand? Yell at her."

"Yes."

"I'm going to stay on the phone. Now you go in there and try to get her up. Scream at her. Just make her get up. Okay, honey?"

"Okay."

Sophia puts down the phone and goes into Lillian's bedroom. She walks to the edge of the bed. She picks up the pill bottle and turns it upside down. Two pills fall out. She picks up the movie magazine which is folded to an article on Marilyn Monroe, looks at it and puts it on the bedside table.

She shakes Lillian hard and screams.

"Mama! WAKE UP!"

Still, Lillian only moans.

She shakes even harder and screams louder.

"MAMA. MAMA, WAKE UP. Pearl is on the phone."

Lillian doesn't respond. Sophia puts her hands on her shoulders and begins to cry, certain now that her mother will never wake up.

"Please, wake up, Mama, please."

Sophia shuffles back to the phone.

"She won't wake up."

"Honey, is she still breathing?"

"Yes"

Pearl takes a deep breath.

"Good. That's real good. Okay. I'm going to hang up and call Sheriff McRae. Do you remember him?"

"Yes."

"He'll come over there and help your mama."

"Are you coming, too?"

"Of course I'm coming. It's going to take me a little while to get there but as soon as I call Uncle Bud, I'll be in my car on the way. Now, honey. Listen to me. I want you to keep your sisters calm. Sit down with them in the living room and watch TV. Tell them your mama is sick but everything is going to be okay. Tell them I am coming."

"Okay."

"I'm hanging up now, honey. You sure you're all right?"

Sophia nods and hangs up the phone.

SOPHIA

Cousin Pearl and her mother arrived just as the rescue workers carried Mama out of the house on a stretcher. I remember she had an oxygen mask on but her eyes were closed. Mama had only one dream in her life and when Daddy took off, I guess he took it with him. I think Mama just couldn't live without a dream and me and my sisters were too much real life for her.

She never did wake up. Cousin Pearl held her hand till the sound of Mama's heartbeat on the monitor slowed and became irregular and then finally quit altogether. Cousin Pearl wouldn't let us in so we never got to say good-bye, but that's for the best, I reckon.

She gave us each a little box that we filled with the red dirt from Mama's grave. She said we should never forget Mama or that we were real red dirt girls and that if things got bad for us, all we had to do was look at our box and remember that.

Since Daddy couldn't be found, we girls went to live with Cousin Pearl. She raised us as if we were hers. At first, we went on tour with her, but after a few years of traveling, Pearl married Kevin, settled down and devoted herself to being our Mama.

Daddy was eventually found living in Seattle with a new family and, with the help of Mr. Drake, we girls recovered all that was due us and more. Cousin Pearl invested some of that money along with the money Little Joe left Mama. In 1999, we put that money to real good use opening the newly built Lillian Dunn Reynolds Women's Center.

Gina and Lola followed in the footsteps of Pearl, becoming Country Music singers. Sometimes, Pearl joins them on tour. Brigitte is an attorney in New York City. She spends her free time helping runaway girls find their dreams. Raquel married a computer software engineer and lives in Charlotte. She writes children's stories. Mr. McDowell passed away last year and Grandma, tired of living alone has finally come home.

And me. I guess I'm like my uncle, Little Joe. I love this red dirt. I reckon it's in my blood. I married a man who loves it as much as me and we settled in on this old farm not too long ago. Now I'm raising my own little tribe of red dirt girls.

I opened the letter from Uncle Joe to Mama and had it framed. It had a simple message I wish Mama had read. It said: "RIDE THE WIND, LIL SIS."

And one more thing before I go. In the shoebox was an old 8mm film roll. I played it the other day.

Mama is running in and out of the water's edge, pant legs rolled up, laughing as a wave catches her. She is running from a crab that Daddy is holding just inside the frame. She runs again toward something she sees in the distance and bends down to pick it up. She rises and turns, face beaming holding up a starfish. And, finally, she stops running, poses like a movie star, throwing kisses to her adoring fans. This is the way I will remember my Mama, as a girl, full of hope and dreams.

COMING SOON!

Tears for the Innocent

Prologue

The townspeople in the valley were afraid of the forest that smothered the nearby hills. No matter It was dark and dense, with a thick canopy of limbs stretching across the sky. Limbs, they whispered, like the arms of the dead, grasping each other in a macabre embrace that denied all but the rarest and hardiest beams of sunlight. No matter as well, the wretched screams that sometimes punctured the eerie silence or the whispered tales of the lost ones: those who entered and never returned.

No, none of this mattered to the people, for theirs was a dark and cruel world. Their small town was cast in darkness by the shadows of the massive stone walls that surrounded it. Their miserable little huts were ink black dark inside with tiny circles of dim, smoky light, emanating from stubs of rancid candles. Death was a companion who lay on a pallet beside the door, unafraid to reveal itself even to those with the most protective charms or the most devout believer.

It was the creeping mist that occasionally oozed from the forest floor that frightened them. It would lick its way toward the town, spreading over the hillside, searching for the unknowing traveler, the young lovers seeking privacy, or, most especially, the child who had lost sight of her mother. Ever closer, it lingered longer with each visit.

"The devil's own breath," they called it and it was coming for them.

The people became more desperate. For life, what there was of it, became unbearable. Families rushed to the safety of their huts and barred their doors from their neighbors. Husbands fought with wives who neglected children crying from the smoke that stung their eyes and the hunger that gnawed at their shrinking bellies.

So when the moon was full and, in particular, when it glowed a warm honey yellow (which had a special, secret but lost meaning), the old women trudged stoically to the top of the hill, to an ancient temple guarded by a witch of the forest. With them, they carried the most powerful charm of the town as an offering - the grease from the rotting body of a hanged man. Encircled by moonlight, they danced naked in a small clearing, their pale, ghostly bodies bowing and swaying to the rhythm of the windblown trees. They chanted bits and pieces of spells barely remembered, spells invoking the spirit of the goddess of the old days. Beyond the circle, in the blackest of darkness, a pair of red eyes glowed, soon followed by another and another until the old women were surrounded by an uncanny ring of blinking red.

They danced until dawn and with the rising light, they saw the wolves behind the red eyes. They fell down, exhausted, content in the knowledge that the old goddess had smiled favorably upon them for, as everyone knew, the wolf was a fortuitous omen.

But still the mist came.

On the day it reached the town, the sun hid behind the moon in fear, or so the people believed. The tailor's wife stabbed her children to death with a pair of dull scissors. Miller beat his wife senseless then turned his ire upon his neighbor, who in turn set fire to Miller's crooked little house. Babies strangled from the choking vapor, their mothers driven into the streets, screaming, insane from helplessness. Pastor Andras huddled in the corner of his plain church, unable to offer comfort to his terrified flock, for he believed, deep in his heart, that he had chosen the wrong faith. He longed for the protection of the gargoyles, for the vivid images of God's justice and mercy that graced the old sanctuary. What more proof did he need? Surely, the end of the world had come and the town was being swallowed by the devil, traveling a sure path to the fiery depths of hell.

ACKNOWLEDGEMENTS

I'd like to thank Ann Lorenz for her patient editing and my best writer friend, Karen Cheesman, for her encouraging and thoughtful comments. This novella has been a long journey and I also want to thank my sister, Cathy Marks, who has been there from the beginning, always insisting that I could actually write this story.

ABOUT THE AUTHOR

Carolyn Haywood was born in Tucson, Arizona to US Air Force parents where she lived for ten days before being whisked away to live the life of a well-traveled gypsy. She began her writing career at age 50 when she started writing award-winning screenplays. She converted her first script, Red Dirt Girls, into a novella in 2018. It is based on the lyrics of the hit song, Red Dirt Girl, by Emmylou Harris and is the poignant tale of a young girl struggling to escape her life of familial abuse, infidelity, drugs, and alcohol. She is currently writing her second novel, Tears for the Innocent, available soon on Amazon.

Made in United States
Cleveland, OH
14 August 2025